I0544356

A WALLFLOWER'S MIDSUMMER NIGHT'S CAPER

REVENGE OF THE WALLFLOWERS MULTI-AUTHOR COLLECTION
BOOK FIFTEEN

ALINA K. FIELD

HAVENLOCK PRESS

COPYRIGHT

Copyright © 2024 Mary J. Kozlowski
ISBN No. 978-1-944063-450

Havenlock Press
PO Box 1891
La Mirada, CA 90637-1891

June 11, 2024

This is a work of fiction. Names, characters, places, and incidents either are the product of the author's imagination or are used fictitiously, and any resemblance to actual persons, living or dead, business establishments, events, or locales is entirely coincidental.

All rights reserved under International and Pan-American Copyright Conventions. No part of this text may be reproduced, transmitted, downloaded, decompiled, reverse engineered, or stored in or introduced into any information storage and retrieval system, in any form or by any means, whether electronic or mechanical, now known or hereinafter invented without the express written permission of the copyright owner, except in the case of brief quotations embodied in critical articles and reviews.

The reverse engineering, uploading, and/or distributing of this book via the internet or via any other means without the permission of the copyright owner is illegal and punishable by law. Please purchase only authorized editions, and do not participate in or encourage electronic piracy of copyrighted materials. Your support of the author's rights is appreciated.

Without in any way limiting the author's exclusive rights under copyright, any use of this publication to "train" generative artificial intelligence (AI) technologies to generate text or speech is expressly prohibited, including without limitation, technologies that are capable of generating works in the same style or genre as this work. The author reserves all rights to license uses of this work for generative AI training and development of machine learning language models.

Cover Design by Dar Albert of Wicked Smart Designs

A WALLFLOWER'S MIDSUMMER NIGHT'S CAPER

A Midsummer Night's masquerade at her family's country home presents the Honorable Nancy Lovelace with the perfect opportunity for revenge against the man who ruined her first London season —a man she's known since childhood, a man she'd once thought she loved. With the help of her crew of younger relatives, she'll give him his comeuppance.

Simon Crayding's newly inherited properties are in disarray, and, thanks to his bad behavior, he's no longer known to society as Captain Crayding but as the Swilling Duke. When an old school chum invites him for a Midsummer Night's party, he jumps at the chance to lick his wounds among friends... as well as to apologize to his friend's sister, Nancy, because apparently, he's done something to hurt her, he just doesn't remember what.

It soon becomes clear that Nancy will not easily

forgive. Never one to resist a challenge—or a beautiful woman—Simon vows to find out why. As the night unfolds and passions rise, will Simon be well and truly punished, or will Nancy be caught in her own game?

CHAPTER ONE

APRIL 1824, LONDON

*T*he Honorable Nancy Lovelace peered out the window of the carriage as they passed rows of elegant townhouses and turned onto Lady Chilcombe's square. Outside a residence across the park, groups of gentlemen shook hands and slapped backs in greeting, while a nearby carriage disgorged far more ladies than the small conveyance ought to hold.

When the Lovelace carriage stopped for traffic, Nancy had a good long look. Now the gentlemen were directing their enthusiastic welcomes to the ladies.

What sort of gathering was that?

"Drat." Mama, the dowager baroness, Lady Neda

Loughton, leaned forward. "I thought we left early enough to avoid traffic."

The brief trip around a corner and down two squares would be over far too soon, and then Nancy would have to, as Mama had said, face her fears.

Now that she finally would have her first season at the ripe age of nineteen, she was determined not to make a hash of it. She would act her part, remember her lines, curtsy on cue, just as though she were presenting a play at school or in her family's ballroom. When she could be someone else and follow a script, she wasn't nervous. But to respond to the unexpected… that was when she tripped all over herself. Literally.

Hands damp in her elbow length gloves, she braced them on the velvet-upholstered seat of her brother Fitz's town carriage, then set one hand upon each knee, and *then* gripped them together in her lap before moving to smooth the skirt of her exquisite new gown. Though her new stays tortured her, the suffering was fair penance for the heavenly frock. The wider skirt was the height of fashion and the pale pink tulle over satin ended in a white and pink rouleaux circling the hem. The pink rouleaux had proven to have a mind of its own though. Her maid, Meg, had repaired some of the stitches before they'd run out the door.

"Nancy." Her mother patted Nancy's hand. "Nerves are normal at your first ball, but you will be fine. Lady Chilcombe is a dear friend, and… and will need our support as well, this being her first ball as a widow."

This was also Mama's first ball since Papa's death; Mama's first trip to London in decades without the late Lord Loughton.

She'd heard Lady Chilcombe's whisper to Mama about widows making a second come-out.

Nancy took her mother's hand. "You're nervous too. You don't need to be."

Mama was petite and trim, and still so lovely. She would be the belle of the ball amongst the older men.

She herself had inherited Mama's blue eyes and blonde hair, but the excessive height that rendered her clumsy and the strong jaw that made strangers think she was stubborn, those had come from her father.

"I do wish one of the boys was with us," Nancy said. She had four brothers old enough to attend a ball and none of them happened to be in town for the start of this, her first season. "Whoever am I going to dance with?"

Mama squeezed her hand back and smiled. "Lady Chilcombe tells me Simon will be there."

A flicker of warmth crept up Nancy's neck and stirred her nerves. The smile on her mother's face turned sly.

Simon Clayding was her brother George's best friend from childhood.

Nancy suppressed a sigh and said tightly, "Simon is a duke now. He won't look below an earl's daughter."

Nor would he remember her, the awkward, clumsy girl who, nine years ago, had followed him around like a puppy.

Oh, but if he did remember her? She'd spent years comparing every one of her suitors against Simon—his looks, of course, but also his humor, his kindness.

Though in retrospect, his treatment of her had been more like sufferance toward a friend's younger sister than kindness.

"Nonsense," Mama said. "You're grown up now and Simon might not recognize you, but he's kept up a correspondence with your brother George, and occasionally with Fitz. He won't cut you. Perhaps he'll even ask you to dance."

The words, uttered just as the coach rolled to a halt and the door opened, sent Nancy reeling. She hopped out before the steps were all the way down. The pink rouleau around her hem took the opportunity to spring free again, and she fell into the arms of a startled, bewigged footman.

NANCY LIFTED HER SKIRTS AND TIPTOED ALONG THE dark passage, willing herself to proceed in a stately manner, with her hem and her hair wreath minding their places.

She had been doing so well, so very, very well, quelling the nervousness twitching through her... Until that first step from the carriage when she'd knocked the poor footman's wig askew.

She took a long breath and assumed the ramrod posture that was her defense against the busk in her stays—as well as all the other worries unsettling her.

The dancing would start soon, and she would *so* love to dance the first set.

There'd be no more tripping. No more ripped clothing. No more embarrassing awkwardness.

If only she and Mama were not virtually alone in this crowd of strangers.

Not that the ball guests were all strangers to her mother. Though Mama had been absent from London these last two years since Papa's death, she'd kept up her correspondence with friends and acquaintances.

Mama would find someone to lead her daughter out. Someone young, Nancy hoped, but not too fashionable. Not eager to wed, because she wasn't at all ready to spend hours drinking tea or being driven in the park. She could drink tea and go for drives at home, and there were far too many interesting museums and theaters in London to waste time on mere courting. Her friend from school, Sally Simpkins, was in London as well, though Mama had advised restraint about socializing with the daughter of a Drury Lane actress, never mind that the woman was considered respectable.

It had seemed a trifle unfair. Sally was as much a lady as any of the *ton*, and she'd know exactly how to act with the crowd gathered here, no matter how high the title.

Oh, for a familiar dance partner. Her brother, George, wouldn't mind if she stepped on his toes; her brother, Fitz, would laugh if she made a wrong turn. The same was true for Rupert and Selwyn.

Or... what about Simon?

Thoughts of him sent emotions spiraling in her, longing twining with annoyance, and strands of hurt and embarrassment befuddling her, so that when she turned a corner, she stumbled against a large body with a startled squeak.

"Here now. What's this?"

Powerful hands matched the deep masculine voice and set her back, steadying her. She looked up, astonished, and her heart swelled and threatened to burst. All the mixed emotions evaporated, and joy flooded her. Dark hair spilled over one blue-gray eye and the full lips pursed together in a frown.

He'd come for her. Simon Clayding—Duke of Something now, but he would always be Simon to her—Simon was here.

"It's you," she said. "I'm so s-sorry. I'm as clumsy as ever. B-but... you're here?"

Perhaps he would dance with her. Perhaps *she* should ask *him*.

"'Course I'm here." He blinked, as though trying to focus. "Question is, why are *you* here looking like a fresh young thing ready for your come-out?"

"S-Simon?"

"*Simon?*" He muttered a foul profanity she'd heard only on the rarest of occasions spilling from one of her brothers' mouths. "Demmed Percy told you my Christian name, I suppose, and sent you along. One of his pranks. Well, madam, you're a pretty thing, and I mean you no offense, but I'm not going to be sidetracked tonight. I'm *not* interested."

A wave of misery stilled her tongue and drove the breath from her. She'd loved Simon Clayding since her brother George brought him home from school that first holiday fifteen years ago when she'd been not much more than a baby.

In the dim light of a wall sconce, his gaze darkened and held hers, despite his proclaimed lack of interest.

Perhaps... Simon hadn't seen her in nine years. He didn't recognize her. He had her confused with someone else.

Reasoning trickled back into her senses, bringing along the strong scent of brandy.

Of course. He was completely foxed.

She licked her lips, preparing to set him straight,

but as she opened her mouth, a spark lit his eyes and turned up the corners of his mouth.

And then he tugged her, pressing his lips to hers, pressing his chest to her… to her…

Breath left her in a whoosh as he angled his mouth over hers, nibbling and then entering her with his tongue, inflaming desire, demanding surrender.

She gripped his broad shoulders but instead of steadying her, their solidness sent heat spinning through her.

Simon was kissing her. *Simon*. The first man to kiss her. At a public ball. He cared for her. He hadn't forgotten. He meant to mar…

"There." He set her back as suddenly as he'd swooped down on her.

A tendril of hair fell over her cheek, the same one that a maid had just pinned.

"That's all you'll get from me. Go back and tell Percy we've had our tumble, if you will, and demand payment from *him*. Get you gone before one of the servants sees you and throws you out on your arse."

He turned her around and smacked her bottom. She staggered against the wall, righted herself, and turned back ready to give him a piece of her mind.

But he'd disappeared.

Percy? Payment? What was he talking about?

"Oh, miss, that lock of hair has fallen again."

The maid who'd seen to her hair eyed the loose tendril. Heat flooded Nancy's cheeks. Had the girl seen that kiss? Or worse, heard what Simon had said?

The maid wrung her hands. "I'll see to it again unless you'd like me to find someone else."

Nancy gathered her wits and shook her head. "It wasn't your fault. Come, I'll follow you back to the retiring room."

And perhaps she'd stay there for the rest of the ball.

* * *

"THAT'S HER."

A cluster of girls turned curious gazes that sent Nancy's heart pounding.

The gloved hand that flew up to cover the speaker's tittering mouth couldn't hide the silly girl's words. Nancy's acute hearing had been honed by years dodging the antics of her siblings.

"Hold up your head, Nancy," Mama said.

Nancy did as she was told while dread slithered down her spine. Lady Chilcombe's ball the week before had engendered a mocking caricature that spurred her family to action. Her maid had reported the comings and goings in the public rooms at Loughton House: curious callers had come sniffing for gossip, Mama's bosom friends had offered aid and sympathy, and even an impudent reporter had tried to worm his way in.

She herself, after one glance at the hideous depiction in the cartoon, had refused to leave her bedchamber until Fitz, who'd rushed to town without his family, barged into her room, cajoling, encouraging, and when all else failed, offering his gentle sort of bullying.

"Shall I go knock their pretty heads together?" Fitz teased.

He'd deigned to accompany them to this rout tonight.

"Better that I should find someone to introduce them to Nancy," Mama said. "Remember what I told you, young lady."

You are The Honorable Nancy Lovelace, Mama had said. *Head up, shoulders back, act as if nothing of any importance has happened.*

Nothing of importance. The one man who ought to have shown her kindness had humiliated her in a very public way. She'd never fancied being a leader of the ton. She'd looked forward to seeing London, meeting an old friend, and dressing up for parties and balls. Just another girl making her come-out.

Simon had given her notoriety, not just amongst the ton, but all the mocking classes that ogled the caricatures slapped up in shop windows. He'd made her a laughingstock.

Across the room, a gaggle of fresh-faced bucks

turned their gazes her way. Mischief glittered in their eyes. *That* she could almost stomach. She had younger brothers, after all. It was the older peacock stuffed into a tight waistcoat advancing on them who made her skin crawl.

Before he could reach them, Mother shooed Fitz toward the fellow and led Nancy off for a round of obligatory introductions. "Remember, this will pass," she whispered.

As the gathering wore on, though, it was clear Mama was wrong. The whispers, winks, and knowing looks pushed Nancy's nerves to the precipice. No one came along at this party to knock her to the floor, and she managed to remain standing, oh yes. But the panic gripping her throat had her croaking the rote conversational platitudes she'd learned as a girl. How she'd survive the rest of this miserable season, she had no idea.

If she ever saw Simon again, she'd wring his neck.

JUNE 1824
Loughton Manor

"THAT ONE LOOKS LIKE BABY HENRY'S BOTTOM."

"Does not. It looks like the vicar's jiggly cheeks when he's pon-ti-fi-cating, doesn't it, Nancy?"

The children's voices carried on the still air as Simon Clayding, Duke of Swillingstone, broke through the apple tree orchard to the lawn. Three figures—a lady and two children aged about seven or eight—lay on the grass.

His breath caught. The lawn sloped down to a wide lake that some prior baron had created by choking the river downstream. Across the water, the white pillars of the estate's folly gleamed in the late morning sun, ringed by lushly blooming roses in shades of pink and red. On this side, sheep grazed peacefully in a nearby field, and the happy children stretched between a lady with soft golden hair, swelling breasts, and long legs ending in trim ankles.

She was Nancy? George, his old school friend, had told him she'd be roaming somewhere in the grounds of Loughton Manor with her niece and nephew.

Dear God, why had he not gone to her straightaway?

She was a mere child in the memories he'd carried with him from his earliest visits to Loughton Manor. From those memories he'd crafted a few dreams for himself: a peaceful home, a large happy family, a prosperous estate. Given the relative poverty of his birth, they had seemed impossible to achieve.

But he was a duke now; perhaps the first two desires were in reach sooner rather than later. He needed an heir, and he'd welcome even more children with the right sort of wife. Prosperity would take longer, but he was willing to work for it.

He'd got off to a bad start with this duke business. This visit was his chance to set things right and begin again.

The little girl plucked the head off a wildflower. "I wish we could visit the folly."

The lady's consoling murmur was too quiet to understand, but mention of the folly stirred more happy memories in Simon. School holidays here had been filled with adventures on the lake and rainy afternoons spent sheltering in the folly.

Designed by some past Lord Loughton, the structure's octagonal portico surrounded a central room with a large hearth. There were other chambers as well: on the main floor, two large, cluttered storerooms; downstairs, kitchen rooms with a pump for fresh water from the folly's rooftop cistern, and even a privy tucked away. Upstairs there were two low-ceilinged rooms with naked bedframes. It was a ramshackle play place for them, but no adults bothered them there.

"Well, we can't, Mary," the boy said. "Uncle Fitz said it's still off limits until the repairs are finished and the bridge is completed."

Simon chuckled. Typical male—pontificating again like the jiggly-cheeked vicar.

"Perhaps your papa will take you there in a few

days, Mary," Nancy said, "if they've finished construction inside the folly. Maybe after the party. If the new bridge isn't ready, you can walk upstream and cross on the old one."

The voice, a low, throaty alto, sent his heart beating unexpectedly faster.

"Or we could go over by the steppingstones upstream," the boy said.

"Have your legs grown long enough?" she teased.

The lad wriggled, shrugging. "Or, we could pull out one of the skiffs from the shed."

"They both have holes. Perhaps after tomorrow night's party, the servants will have time to mend them. Now look." She pointed at the sky. "Those, Benjamin, are cumulus clouds. And those..." She pointed westward "are cirrhus."

"I like the fat ones better," Benjamin said.

Simon walked closer, shuffling through the grass to make as much noise as possible. "And let us hope we do not have nimbus clouds for tomorrow night's party," he said.

Nancy lifted her head and looked back. Grass clung to her hair. She sat up, stumbled to her feet, and steadied herself on the boy's shoulder. Taller than most women and many men, she looked even better standing up. The thin summer gown clung to her legs and outlined a shapely figure that made his mouth grow dry and manly parts stir. This was Nancy, but not the thin, startled figure of the scandal sheet. She looked more like... like someone else, but he couldn't quite grasp *who*.

She certainly wasn't that skinny little girl who'd rushed out in her nightgown to wish him a tearful goodbye when he'd left to return to his regiment. She'd grown into a woman—a delectable one—since he'd last seen her.

Or, since he last *remembered* seeing her.

She whacked her bonnet on her wrinkled skirt and clamped it on her head, dislodging a few blonde tendrils and blades of grass, then scrutinized him through narrowed eyes, their icy blue challenging him.

He thought back to his last visit to Loughton Manor, when she was not much bigger than the two who were inspecting him just as closely. It was her sister, Cassandra, who'd been the greater hoyden. Nancy had followed along, the quiet one, the gentle, awkward one, and on that last visit so many years ago, the one with adoring eyes.

There was no adoration in her gaze now. She'd had her first whirl on the marriage mart at the age of nineteen and had come home miserable, depressed and angry.

And it was Simon's fault, her brother George said.

She'd appeared in the scandal sheets as an awkward wallflower, grossly insulted by the greatest cad of the Season. Himself.

He supposed that the title of greatest cad was quite an achievement since he'd only attended that one ball after taking up the title of the Duke of Swillingstone.

The previous duke, as it turned out, had been a far distant cousin. Inheriting the title and all the trappings that went with it had seemed like an incredible stroke of luck, resembling something out of a fairytale. Simon's mother had been a farmer's daughter. His father had worked as a clerk—related to a duke of course—but their branch of the family tree had drooped lower with every generation.

The other branches had thinned as well, at least of male progeny.

To Simon's surprise, he'd discovered that he, a captain who'd barely scraped together the blunt for mess fees and uniforms, was the new duke. He'd immediately left the army and swanned into London.

And then learned just how much lay on his ducal shoulders, and how much of the ducal resources the previous incumbent had frittered away.

There were numerous holdings: a townhouse in Mayfair, a great pile of an abbey in Derbyshire, another manor in Sussex, hunting lodges in various locales, stables and kennels, now almost empty. All of them had leaky roofs, crumbling mortar, and serious problems with dry rot.

Not to mention the problems with the tenants' dwellings.

There was also a mortgage on each unentailed property, as well as personal loans, all with payments due by the midsummer quarter.

His time in London had been brief, but, er, *colorful*. The late duke's solicitor and all of Simon's attentive new friends at his new clubs insisted the only course was to marry an heiress, a notion that stuck in his craw.

Despite his reluctance, he'd rigged himself out in a new suit of evening clothes—on credit, of course—and found his way to Lady Chilcombe's ball in Grosvenor Square. It promised to be dazzling, filled with young virgins eager to wear a duchess's coronet. Two of them were particularly wealthy, one the daughter of an industrialist, the other the daughter of a colonial planter who'd made a fortune in the sugar trade. All he had to do was pick one.

So, he'd looked at the account books, swallowed his misgivings, and gone. He'd stopped at White's for some bottled courage, and then moved on to Boodle's for a bit more. There'd been another stop at a private gentleman's party, and then his arrival at Lady Chilcombe's.

And there, he'd been rude. He'd been careless. But mostly he'd been drunk; blind drunk, falling down drunk, passing out drunk. Plus, he'd apparently bashed his head in his meeting with the floor—whilst knocking over a young lady.

This young lady, the one spearing him with her icy glare.

The wits had christened him The Swilling Duke.

When he was finally able to crawl from his bed two days later, the caricature reached him. He'd called for the traveling chaise he'd inherited and the efficient valet, also inherited, and fled London, flat on his back in the conveyance's rigged up bed and still with a throbbing head.

He'd needed to tour his estates anyway. And in the weeks since the party, he had—every blessed one of them, except for the castle in Scotland and the villa in the south of France.

It was a whirlwind of short visits, mere days to review the books, tour the properties, and meet with the estate managers. Too short to say yes to the invitations to dinners and local assemblies. Not that there were many of those, given the reputation that followed him.

On the second week of his estate tour, after a day spent going over the accounts at Routheston Abbey, he'd got up the nerve to pull out the caricature and study it. It was a farce in two parts. In the first square, two ladies with shocked expressions looked at a third figure, a grotesque version of himself. On the left, a dark-haired young lady stood covering her mouth, her eyes wide. On the right, a blonde-haired young lady held up her hands, warding him off.

In the second square, the grotesque jackanapes was sprawled atop the blonde.

A face like his victim's had registered somewhere in his boggy brain. The cartoonist identified her as Miss N. L., but he couldn't dredge up an N. L. from the females he'd met in London, and the only blonde baggage he did vaguely remember from that night... well, she hadn't been an N. L. Her name had been something like Katie, Tilly, Bessy. Fetching, well-dressed, pretty, even, and completely available for the right price.

By the time he'd left Routheston, he'd laid hands on a scandal sheet and discovered that Miss N.L was the youngest sister of Lord L from Leicestershire.

The Lord L. who owned this bit of paradise where Simon had found a home.

That same day, he'd posted a letter of apology to Fitzhenry Lovelace, Lord Loughton.

No reply had reached him on his travels, not even a forwarded letter. Fitz, instead, sent an emissary. George Lovelace, one of Fitz's many younger brothers, and Simon's best friend from school, arrived unexpectedly at Simon's last stop, his property near Marston Green.

Nancy brushed her skirts again, and his mouth watered.

The caricaturist had caught the basics—a slim

figure, trim ankles, abundant fair hair. There was no look of shock in her eyes now, only the sort of fierce disdain he'd received from a few of the aristocratic officers among the higherups.

The shy little girl had grown into a beautiful woman.

"Miss Nancy," Simon said, bowing, "it is I, Simon Clayding. Surely you remember me."

She watched him, unsmiling, and after a long pause, dipped her head and said, "Your grace. Children, make your bow and curtsy to the duke."

They each sent her a look, eyed him curiously, and did as they were told.

Then nothing.

"I'm here for the Midsummer Night's party," he said, filling the silence.

She tilted her head, still observing him.

"George, invited me."

"Are you a friend of my stepfather, George Lovelace?" the little boy asked. "I am Benjamin Halverton. My brother is the Earl of Glanford."

"And I am the Honorable Mary Anastasia Lovelace," the little girl said. "My father is Lord Loughton."

Simon bowed. "I'm very pleased to meet both of you, and to see you again, Miss Nancy."

Nancy looked away.

Mary tugged at her skirt. "Why are you angry with him?" she said in a stage whisper.

"Angry with whom?" Nancy sounded bored. She turned away again, shaded her eyes, and a grin lit her face. "Do excuse me."

Picking up her skirts, she ran, her ankles and legs distracting Simon, until he noticed a male figure hurrying to meet her, his loose neckcloth flapping.

"Excuse us too," Benjamin said, running off.

"Good day to you, your grace." Mary wobbled another curtsy and hurried after them.

When Nancy hugged the vagabond fellow, a spurt of jealousy hit Simon so fiercely he would have punched him if he'd been standing with them.

And he just might anyway. He swallowed his pride and his sudden anger and hurried to join the group.

CHAPTER TWO

*N*ancy smiled sweetly at the man seated to her left, the circumspect, middle-aged Mr. Smith. The dear man had been inherited by Nancy's sister-in-law And Fitz's wife. Mary Elizabeth, Lady Loughton, known as Mel to the family, had acquired Mr. Smith upon the death of her grandfather, Gregory Sawley, along with the Sawley Bank and a tremendous personal fortune.

Mr. Smith was a safe and pleasant dining companion. Nancy had, so far, completely ignored the man to her right.

The pompous prig.

Seated further down the table, Nancy's mother, the dowager Lady Loughton, was sending meaningful looks whenever she happened to glance her way. Sooner or later, she would have to allow herself to be spoken to by the Swilling Duke, or God forbid, speak words to him herself.

Mama didn't agree with holding grudges. Mama thought that problems between two people ought to be discussed and resolved. But there was no "between two people" with her and the Swilling Duke. He'd utterly ruined her first season.

Oh, how she'd looked forward to finally seeing London. She would tolerate the balls, routs and picnics for Mama's sake, and relish the museums, musicales, shopping and especially the theater.

She'd looked forward to seeing her school friend, Sally Simpkins. But Mama had been so angry about Nancy's lack of enthusiasm, she'd claimed there'd been some whispering about Sally's mother, a famous, successful, and generally respectable actress. Mama had absolutely refused any visits with Sally.

Fortunately, she'd run into Sally one day at Hatchard's. They'd been able to arrange a clandestine correspondence via Nancy's maid, Meg.

Now, Sally was in Birmingham, where her mother was whiling away the summer at the Theatre Royal, before traveling on to France and Italy for a European tour. Birmingham was not *so* far away, and there was even a chance, Sally said, that Nancy might be able to accompany them on their upcoming travels. Mrs. Simpkins had written to Mama in early June, inviting her and Nancy for a visit. Mama had written back declining the invitation.

Nancy had begged her to reconsider, but not even Mel had been supportive. And George's wife, Sophie? She was a female version of practical George.

Running away was the only option—which Nancy knew would not be the act of a dutiful daughter, would probably hurt Mama's feelings, and would ruin her own reputation.

As if her reputation would matter if she could join the world of the theater.

"I say, your grace," Cassandra said, "are you looking forward to taking your place on the London stage as the newest young eligible duke?"

Trust her sister, Simon's loud dining companion on the other side, to find a way to chide Nancy.

Cassandra knew Sally as well. They'd all met at Mrs. Thomas's school, which was open to respectable girls of all classes. Cass's best friend there had been Charlotte Cartwright, whose father was in trade. Nancy's best friend had been Sally, who'd been her champion in overcoming her shyness by walking the boards, at least at school and in the Lovelace home theatricals.

Nancy had dreamed of an introduction to the theater world during her season. The prospect of meeting eligible suitors in London had been last on her list, until she'd learned that Simon would be in town.

And look how that had turned out.

A loud laugh came from the juvenile end of the table where her brother James and George's stepson, Arthur, Earl of Glanford, were regaling the others about their trip to Lancashire and the plans for the railway that would cut through Arthur's property.

She had wanted to accompany them on that visit and spend time with Sophie, George's wife and Arthur's mother. But Fitz and Mel had needed to travel to London for a meeting of the bank's board, their nursery maid had been down with a bad summer cold, and Mother had needed Nancy's help with the children.

She sighed, listening to Mr. Smith's tale of his visit to the new National Gallery, which she hadn't had a chance to visit. She had no more than an average interest in art, but she'd love to return to London and see the sights without the social pressure of the Season.

When Jeffrey, their footman, brought around the next course, she caught her mother's steady gaze. Good manners would require her to turn and speak to the Swilling Duke.

Gritting her teeth, she studied her plate. Despite this being a family dinner, Mama had brought out the best chinaware for her illustrious guest.

Let *him* make the first move.

"Are you interested in art, Miss Nancy?"

As his deep baritone rolled through her, she *sensed*, rather than *saw* him looking at her. Heat crept up her neck. He'd been eavesdropping.

She shrugged. "As one is, your grace."

The footman filled his wine glass and he sipped. "A good burgundy," he said, "though I'm no expert on wines."

"Who counts quality, when one goes for quantity?" she murmured.

A moment she could only describe as stunned silence passed, compelling her to look.

Her throat tightened, her heart thrummed, and she felt the onset of the awkwardness she'd suffered as a child. Simon looked even more polished than he had that afternoon in the open field. He *looked* like a *duke*, as if he'd been born to it, which she supposed he had been.

His brown curls—natural, she remembered—lay artlessly at his temples and tickled the top of his elegantly tied neckcloth at the back. His eyes glowed a dark silver as he looked down the high bridge of his nose. Squint lines fanned from the corners of his eyes and an old scar traced one cheek.

She was *not* attracted to him. She was *not, not, not*.

She wasn't a child anymore.

Another loud guffaw resounded. "That's enough, James," said her brother Fitz. He had arranged the boys near his place at the head of the table, the better to keep them in line. "Save that rowdiness for the officers' mess."

The duke's lips quirked. "I was surprised this afternoon to see how much James had grown. I remember him toddling around in an infant dress. He's as tall as you."

A reminder of her great height.

"Is James going into the army?"

"Yes, your grace."

He winced. Was he uncomfortable with the title? She'd use it more often then. "Though what they'll do with such a nodcock, I have no idea. Your grace."

He sighed. "If he's a nodcock, he'll fit right in."

She bristled at that. If her little brother ever humiliated a girl the way the duke had her, she'd thrash him to within an inch of his life.

"Though we vanquished Napoleon," he said, "good men are still needed. We're fighting right now in Burma and Africa. There are always wars."

A shadow had passed over him, and she remembered he had fought in the Peninsular campaign. Then, after his last visit nine years ago, he'd gone straight from Loughton Manor to Deal, and from there to Ostend and Brussels. She'd worried herself sick and waited on pins and needles until the Waterloo casualty lists were posted.

"So, Miss Nancy, tell me about your first season."

Her heart lurched. He'd been plucking her heart strings, churning up reminders that he'd been a soldier. He'd been at war. The poor, suffering, Swilling Duke.

The ass. The absolute ass.

On the other side of him, Cassandra leaned over her plate and flashed Nancy a warning look.

Cassandra's season that spring had been great fun for her. Having met and married a viscount the autumn before—in somewhat scandalous circumstances, though no one would discuss it— Cass had all the freedom of a new bride and none of the nerves of an unsettled girl. Marriage, though, had made her bossier and more overbearing than ever.

Nancy signaled to Biggs, their butler, who came and filled her wine glass. As she moved to set the glass on the table, an opportune guffaw came from the juvenile section, distracting the diners. She fumbled with the glass, it tipped, and the good vintage spilled all over the Swilling Duke.

"You ought to go and change that coat, Swillingstone." Fitzhenry Lovelace, Lord Loughton, held out his tumbler for George to refill.

While a servant sponged the coat, Simon made a quick change of shirt, neck cloth, and waist coat, and returned to the table before dessert. When it was time for the ladies to withdraw, Fitz's wife suggested that since there were only four gentlemen, Saulsfield not arriving until the morrow, that they might wish to withdraw to the library for their port. There was no reason to rush; the ladies would not be waiting in the drawing room. They'd be shuffling the younger members off to bed and otherwise making plans for the party the following night.

Smith had begged off, needing to see to some work, but Simon and his old school friends gathered in front of the hearth in the small masculine room crammed with books.

Simon covered his own glass and shook his head. He'd resolved to stay within limits.

"I only brought one set of evening clothes." He only *owned* one set of evening clothes and he hadn't yet paid off that tailor's bill, a worry that fitted well with his farmer grandfather's inclinations.

George took the chair next to his. "Then we'd best tell Mother not to seat you next to Nancy again." He laughed. "Did you see Mother's face? She'll no doubt pull James aside—a regular occurrence as many times as he's been sent down from school. But *his* lecture will be shorter tonight, thanks to Nancy and her *clumsiness*."

Clumsiness indeed. Simon had caught the look of satisfaction on her face, and despite a moment's irritation, he'd almost laughed.

"What did you say to her, your grace?" Fitz asked.

"Spare me the your-gracing, your lordship."

Simon wrinkled his nose, dodging the question. "I don't know what's worse: being called Swillingstone or *your grace*."

"I suspect Swilling Duke is worse," George said.

He swiped a hand through his hair. "That damned caricature."

"Fortunately, there was only the one mentioning Nancy," Fitz said. "You left town before you could fall on more virgins. Or perhaps," Fitz grinned, "Mel paid off the caricaturist."

Fitz's wife was outrageously rich, having inherited her grandfather's personal wealth and estates and a controlling share in his bank. Somehow, the grandfather had put the money and shares under her control, not Fitz's.

George lounged back in his chair. "Of all the young ladies attending the ball, the only one mentioned in other cartoons was Miss Dalrymple."

"Her wealth came directly from slavery," Fitz said. "Not just from sugar but from the trade in humans as well. Perhaps the artist is an abolitionist."

Simon's grip on his glass tightened. He'd served in the West Indies and seen the plantations. "I suppose it's no fault of the girl that her wealth came from such, but I'll scratch her from my list."

"As I recall, Miss Dalrymple is snatched up already," Fitz said.

"Miss Hazelton is still unmarried," George said. "In fact, Sophie has an acquaintance with the family through her late father, and Mel has invited her. She'll arrive for the party tomorrow night. So there, Simon. Another chance at a fat dowry."

He shook his head. "No. I won't pursue a girl just for her money. I've had a look at almost all my properties. There's plenty of money coming in, just more going out to pay debts and the mortgages."

The previous duke and his wife had been curst extravagant.

"I've put economies in place everywhere." He'd discussed that with George during the Marston Green visit. "I'll be selling some of the unentailed properties and tearing down some of the structures before they collapse, selling the useful bits and pieces. I'm looking at everything: assays for minerals, hunting fees, and even, as you suggested, the potential for railway leases, George."

George nodded. "Good man."

"When you have a clearer picture, speak to Mel about mortgages," Fitz said. "She might have some ideas for you. No promises of course."

He suppressed a shudder. Speaking to a woman about his finances seemed so vulgar. In fact, the thought of speaking to a woman about anything had been difficult lately, with his reputation preceding him.

"Thank you, Fitz." He pondered his remaining brandy and then drank it down.

"More brandy?" George asked.

Simon shook his head. "Good of you to invite me to this party. I'd like to make amends. If only I knew what I did to ruin Nancy's Season, besides what was depicted in that caricature. Surely, she might have laughed off my, er, crudeness, perhaps even gained some attention from eligible suitors. Do you know?"

The brothers exchanged glances.

"Have you remembered anything since we last spoke?" George asked.

"It's fuzzy. I apparently bashed my head and suffered a mild concussion."

"You should ask Nancy," Fitz said.

"I broached the subject of her season tonight at dinner and this was her reply." He pointed to a mottled streak in his dark coat.

Both brothers broke out in laughter.

"Not funny. Won't you tell me now?"

In his visit to Marston Green, George had broached the subject of Nancy's unhappiness, just after he'd extended this Midsummer Night's invitation and before he'd abruptly departed.

"We weren't at Lady Chilcombe's ball, as it happens," Fitz said. "But I can tell you that after that evening, Nancy was wretched. She begged Mother to let her avoid balls and routs, and when Mother refused, she retreated into awkwardness. As you say, she gained attention, mostly from fellows with pockets to let who were after not only her dowry but also family access to my wife's bank. More than one fellow approached asking permission to court her. The two I allowed to propose she turned down."

"Rather rudely, I hear." George laughed. "Slapped one of them when he kissed her."

"Good for her." The notion of Nancy being kissed by some cad, being married to a fortune hunter, riled him.

He glanced at Fitz to find him studying him over his brandy snifter.

"Nancy had a friend from school she wanted to call on," Fitz said, "but Mother thought the girl was not quite the thing. Nancy moped for days over that. Thereafter, the only excursions she seemed to relish were to the theater and museums."

"We thought she'd outgrown her shyness. Nancy's avid for amateur theatricals," George said. "Always organizing our Christmas pantomimes and impromptu family plays."

The young Nancy Simon knew would only sing with her sister and stumbled through pieces on the pianoforte while her brothers sat in their chairs smirking. He'd been among that lot.

Though at his last visit, that Easter Sunday, her yeomanlike attempt at *Sheep May Safely Graze* had touched him so much that the treacly tune had played in his head all the way across the Channel and lowlands and twanged in his head before battle.

"You might ask Mother about your offensive behavior," George said. "She won't speak about it to us. I gather that there were two different, er, incidents. Mother was across the room dancing for the first one." He sat back and grinned. "Note that, Fitz. Our mother danced twice that night with Lindhorst."

Fritz frowned. "That rakehell? He's ten years younger than Mother."

"Eight. And widowed last year. But I digress. The second offense, Simon… well, everyone saw that, I'm told, and you must have been severely concussed if you have little memory of it."

He rubbed the spot on his head that still ached occasionally. "Tell me."

Fitz sat forward in his chair. "Are you being coy, your grace?"

He had the caricature, Percy Nacton's teasing, and a faint recollection as references. "No." He pounded the arm of his chair, stood, and walked to the mantel. "Deuce take it, I was foxed. Completely jug bitten. I left town almost immediately, plunged into work, shut down the wags before they could spew their venom, and before I had to issue a challenge. Demme, I even refused to appear for local assemblies and dinners at my estates. So, no."

"You ducked your head in the sand, old man," Fitz said.

Simon's hands clenched and his pulse pounded in his ears.

"Sit down," George said. "No need to pick a fight

with his lordship tonight. Think man, you're angry now, but Nancy has been fuming for months."

He set his glass on the mantel and faced them. He hadn't ducked his head in the sand—he'd been working, carrying out the duties of a duke. Seeing to his estates and the people who looked to him for their incomes and livelihoods.

Still, a little voice niggled. George was an old friend. He ought to have done more than write to Fitz and wait for a reply. He ought to have sought George out. Perhaps even a duke had to face gossip.

Or, *especially* a duke.

"Tell me what you heard, George."

George nodded. "You were staggering into the supper room with Miss Hazelton all but holding you up, when Nancy passed by and you stumbled into her. 'This chit again,' you said, and proceeded to cast up your accounts all over my sister's new ball gown. And then you collapsed like a felled tree, taking Nancy down in the process."

"Smashed your head on a pillar on the way down," Fitz said. "Thus your memory loss."

This chit again. The girl in the cartoon had seemed familiar.

"For some reason, our little sister, who is as pretty as the next young girl—isn't she George?— had only danced twice, and those times with old codgers who were Mother's friends. And after your, er, christening, she had to leave the ball. Not just any

35

ball, but her very first ball of her very first season. We've tried to tell her there's always next year."

"Sir Percy Nacton told the story at the club," Fitz said. "Thought I might have to challenge him after he had everyone at White's in stitches, but Mel convinced me not to be ridiculous. Friend of yours?"

"From the regiment." Percy had been the most pushing of his friends about attending Lady Chilcombe's ball. In fact, he'd had Simon wheedle an invitation for him.

He felt the blood draining from his head and returned to his chair. Sweet, kind, gentle Nancy... Damn, but he needed to make amends with her.

He remembered her as a child; George had teased him that she was half in love with him, that she'd be there for him when she grew up.

Gentle-hearted, steady Nancy, who'd grown to be beautiful Nancy with her golden hair and blue eyes.

He gritted his teeth. He knew his way around women, and with Nancy, he had the advantage of her childish infatuation. He'd make amends and more, if she'd allow it. As a rule, he preferred women with a little fire in them, but a duke picking a wife was a different matter. Once Nancy had forgiven him and was restored to her normal, easy self, she'd be just the sort of wife for him: quiet and adoring. He'd offer to court her, and if she was willing, he'd make her his duchess.

"Nacton's a neighbor now," Fitz said. "Inherited an estate in Leicestershire. Sad little place. He'll be at the party tomorrow looking for a dowry."

"Wonderful," Simon said. "Miss Hazelton will be there for him."

"She won't be the only girl with a fat dowry," Fitz said. "Nancy stayed for the whole Season; Mother insisted. When they returned to Loughton Manor and Mel saw how downhearted Nancy was, Mel increased Nancy's dowry to fifty thousand pounds."

"Fifty thous…" It was a larger dowry than Miss Hazelton's. Simon wished they hadn't told him. It sullied his intentions.

"Rich as Croesus is my lady," Fitz said proudly.

"And generous, within prudent bounds," George said. "I say, Simon…"

George smiled over his brandy glass, "Would *you* court Nancy? She has some acceptable suitors among the local landholders, and then of course there's Nacton. I'd just as soon someone push him out of the way."

CHAPTER THREE

*S*imon's hands curled into fists again. *"Nacton is courting her?"*

One cold December at the winter camp in Frenada, he and Nacton had vied for the attentions of the fair Margarita. Percy had won her and then spent the rest of the winter in bed—with a thorough dose of the clap.

Percy Nacton won't have Nancy.

"I recall that you were a dab hand at charming ladies when we were younger," George said.

Simon had been a favorite of the widows around the regiment, and he'd looked forward to a few years of fun as a duke before choosing a wife and begetting an heir. But since Lady Chilcombe's ball, he'd abstained from females of any sort.

"She couldn't do better than a duke," Fitz said. "In

fact, it would be rather nice to have a duke in the family."

"And we know your character," George said. "I saw right away when I visited you that Lady Chilcombe's ball was a one-time faux pas."

"Brought on by the shock of gaining the title," Fitz said.

"And an excess of spirits," George added.

Fitz nodded. "As I said. Shock and the spirits."

"I'm astonished. I have your permission to court her?"

Both brothers nodded.

"If you're sincere," George said. "The Simon I knew wouldn't toy with a young girl's heart, at least, not on purpose."

His head swam like he was suffering an excess of spirits now. So, George's visit to Marston Green had been a kind of interview. He and Fitz had brushed aside his insult to Nancy and were willing to welcome him back to the family on an even more intimate level.

Fitz lifted the brandy bottle. "One more to clear your head?" he asked.

"No." He'd best get his wits about him and stay as sober as possible, at least until he'd secured Nancy's forgiveness. "Court Nancy," he mused instead. "Will she forgive me?"

"Nancy's always been in love with you," Fitz said.

"Which is probably why she's so angry. She'll come around."

George looked doubtful. "Nancy has depths of stubbornness I never saw before."

"Yes." Fitz chuckled. "She and Mother had quite the row two weeks ago about visiting her friend Sally in Birmingham. Mrs. Simpkins' daughter."

"The actress?" Simon cried. "Nancy was at school with an actress?"

"With her daughter," Fitz said. "Don't look so shocked. The mother is a respectable thespian and opera singer, and the daughter, as far as we know, is not treading the boards. Mrs. Simpkins is said to take great pains over her own reputation, and that of her daughter. The mother is leaving in a few weeks for a tour of France and Italy, taking her daughter along. Nancy's visit wouldn't be lengthy. Still, Mother didn't care to chaperone her, and didn't think it wise to send her into Mrs. Simpkins' care, given the size of her new dowry."

"There's no risk of Nancy treading the boards either," George said, "though she does relish our amateur theatricals."

Shy Nancy acting in plays? He'd like to see that for himself.

George leaned back in his chair and frowned. "It would ease matters if you cared for her, Simon."

George had confided that his Sophie's first husband, the Earl of Glanford, had married her only for her dowry, and then promptly squandered the money on gambling and mistresses.

"I… I remember her fondly as a gentle soul," Simon said. Gentle souls had never really appealed to him.

He thought of the way her thin summer gown had clung to her legs and the shapely figure beneath. Gentle or not, it wouldn't be difficult to bed her.

Surely Nancy, after an apology on his part, would come around. He was fit and handsome enough, and he was a duke.

"Fondness," Fitz said. "That's a start, as Mother would say."

"Speaking of Mother," George said, "You must get her on your side, Simon, and you'll be battling uphill there."

He'd done that before: battled uphill, downhill, across bloody fields and rivers. The French had been much more of a challenge than reviving Nancy's childhood tendre and winning her forgiveness and her hand could possibly be. And Lady Loughton had always been kindness itself.

"That's settled," Fitz said. "Now, Cassandra has plagued me with her scheme of employing *A Midsummer Night's Dream* for this party. It's to be a masquerade costume ball. We won't have all the characters, of course, unless we can find someone willing to wear that fellow's donkey ears… what is the character's name?"

"Bottom," George said.

"Yes. Bottom's donkey ears." Fitz grinned. "Cass has already claimed the queen and king of the fairies for herself and Saulsfield, but you, my friend, will be Lysander to Nancy's Hermia."

"Refresh my memory of the play," Simon said.

"Lysander loves Hermia, and Hermia loves him."

Now he remembered. "Nancy is willing?" he asked.

"She doesn't know. Cass will tell her."

Simon rubbed his jaw. "Perhaps *I* should wear the donkey's ears. I've been enough of an ass. Or, I could play Puck."

"James will play Puck," Fitz said.

George chuckled. "We're in for it then. Schoolboy tricks and hijinks. Beware."

"What of the other couple," Simon asked, "the star-crossed lovers—she loves him, he loves Hermia?"

"Demetrius and Helena." Fitz gazed at the fire, a small smile forming. "Why not Miss Hazelton and Sir Percy Nacton?"

He felt another spark of jealousy. "Does Nancy favor Nacton?"

Fitz laughed out loud, but it was George who spoke. "Loathes him. He was there that night as well, remember?"

If only he could.

* * *

"PUT AWAY THAT LETTER AND FIND A COSTUME."

Nancy stuck out her tongue at Cassandra and then grimaced, swiping at cobwebs descending from the rafters, careful of the fragile paper she'd unearthed from an ancient box.

While the men retired for port and conversation, Cassandra had prodded her upstairs to search out costumes. Dusty trunks, crates, and cloth-covered furniture cluttered the attics of Loughton Manor. Nancy had chased her younger brothers up here often enough when they were children, in the days when life was more carefree, and they'd all looked through many of the trunks, finding costumes for their family theatricals. But they'd never made it back to this corner.

"Ooh." Cassandra moved her lantern closer to a maroon leather trunk with brass fittings and rummaged. "Here's a treasure trove."

Nancy glanced over. Rich fabrics shimmered in the light, smelling of the ancient lavender sachets buried with them.

Another time, she would have been giddy with the fun of exploring and dressing up, of a Midsummer Night's party with family and neighbors. After all, for the last few years, she'd been the director and sometimes playwright for the pantomimes and dramas that'd helped fight the boredom of country life.

Another time, this would have been fun, but not now, not with the Swilling Duke swanning around in his handsome arrogance.

"I'd rather not attend this party." Nancy turned away, pulled her lantern closer and studied the spidery feminine writing of the letter she'd discovered. "Perhaps I'll have a megrim tomorrow night."

"I'll never forgive you. This masquerade was my idea, you know, and if my own sister won't support me..."

Drama and bullying. Next Cassandra would go crying to Mama; and Mama, who had seated Nancy next to *him* on purpose at dinner would lecture her a second time this night.

"Fine," she said with a shooing motion, and read on.

Be careful what you wish for.

Have your revenge, if you will, little Wallflower. Give his lordship his comeuppance if you must at the masquerade. I've read the bard too and I see what's afoot—mistaken identity, potions, malicious little fairies, and at the end... Child, I was young once and I know that a gel who sets a trap will fall into it herself, mark my word.

Cassandra squealed and held up a gauzy golden gown, cut in the old style. "This will be mine. I'm to be Titania, the fairy queen. But shh, don't tell anyone."

"And let me guess, Saulsfield will be Oberon, your king."

Cass tittered gleefully. "I will not say."

Nancy glanced at the note again. Deciphering the name inscribed would require better light, but the date listed was a century before.

Who might have sent it? And to whom? Lovelace ladies were the epitome of staid and proper. Well, except perhaps for Cassandra, who'd been a bit wild before she met Saulsfield.

"What is that?"

Nancy hastily slipped the paper into the book where she'd found it. "A journal, I believe. Whose, I don't know. I can't make out the execrable scrawl."

"One of our male ancestors then." Cassandra held up another gown. This one had a dingy white bodice and skirt sprinkled with pink flowers, with an abundance of cloth for old fashioned side hoops. There was even a beaded stomacher. "What do you think?"

It was hideous. "For me? Who am I to play?"

"You are to be Hermia. You must look the virginal young beauty who Lysander and Demetrius both adore."

She'd rather play Puck. She rubbed her forehead.

"Eek, silly. You've got dirt all over yourself." Cass poked at her with a handkerchief. "Look, I know you were crushed in London in the spring." She bestowed a tender, patronizing smile. "'But the duke was drunk when he tossed up his accounts. It's what gentlemen do. He didn't mean to hurt you."

Her jaw ached as she fought another bout of rising anger. Cassandra didn't know what he'd done, what he'd said. She had fled to the retiring room in a panic both times until Mother came to retrieve her.

"The course of true love never did run smooth, little sister.'"

Her hand itched to deliver a smack. Pompous, arrogant, condescending; Lady Saulsfield should just shut her trap.

The rest of them ought to as well.

Various members of the family had condoled with her over her disastrous first ball, and her lack of success in her first London season. Her sister-in-law, Mel, had gone so far as to increase her dowry, though no one had told her by how much, but she didn't care. She wouldn't buy a husband. She wouldn't have a man who only wanted her for her money. How could she ever trust him? She'd never endure another Marriage Mart, though her mother and brothers would try to force her.

Running away seemed the only answer, at least for now.

She pulled out the cryptic letter and reread the lines.

"But I have a surprise," Cassandra whispered.

She quickly shoved the letter back in the book while Cassandra gave her a one-armed hug.

"*He* will be Lysander."

Cassandra's triumphant giggle told Nancy who *He* was.

"After the unmasking, you'll walk into supper on *his* arm. *He* won't be able to ignore you, and you must not spill anymore wine. The course of love did not go smoothly between Lysander and Hermia, but in the end…" A frown creased her sister's brow. "Not that you, of all people, would be able to manage a duchess's coronet. No, that won't be. But at least you will get some revenge."

Nancy gritted her teeth. If she must play Hermia to *his* Lysander, the course of love would not go smoothly. Or at all.

She forced a smile, reminding herself to display a ladylike calm. *Revenge was a dish best served cold.* "Who will James come as?"

"Puck." Cassandra laughed. "And Mother told him there must not be too many ridiculous pranks. And *I* told him, it was I who convinced her to allow him to take part in the masquerade."

James was only fourteen, but he was a master sneak and practical joker.

Their next brother after him, Edward, was only a

little less mischievous. There'd been a question whether Edward would be let out of the schoolroom for the evening's party. In fact, all the children wanted to come, except for George's and Fitz's infant sons.

An idea began to form. Why shouldn't the younger members of the Lovelace clan be there?

Their parents—her mother, her brothers, their wives—would have fits. But a Midsummer Night's masquerade needed magic, and magic needed fairies and goblins.

And revenge, sweet revenge.

She didn't need to be careful what she wished for, just how she went about it. Fall into her own trap? No, indeed.

On the other hand, she'd best have the escape plan she'd been plotting in place. A bag packed with just a few items—Sally had a fabulous wardrobe. Sally could loan her some of her things. She had already researched the coach times. And she had enough funds for the fare to Birmingham, a trip she could make in one long day.

She set the journal aside and surprised Cassandra by throwing herself into the costume hunt.

* * *

"Careful, Mary and Benjamin." Simon spoke with quiet urgency and glanced over at George, who was concentrating on his fishing line and oblivious to the children's antics.

Last night before retiring, Simon, George, and Fitz had agreed on this early morning expedition to the stream running through the Loughton Manor estate. Nancy, the brothers said, usually walked in the early morning before breakfast, and they might run into her.

Fitz had sent word that morning begging off, and they'd picked up two escapees from the nursery on the way downstairs.

"I've got a nibble," George murmured.

Upstream from them, Mary and Benjamin had set aside their fishing poles and were hopping across the rocks that had spanned the water above the lake for as long as Simon could remember.

"George, they might fall in."

"Ha," George breathed out the word and carefully pulled in a small chub. "There's our wager won," he said. "First catch of the morning. You may pay up later. Or you may break even by catching something bigger."

"The children might fall in. Aren't you worried?"

George shrugged. "They both swim."

"Even Mary?"

"Don't you remember? Probably you don't because you were always the first one across the lake. You didn't notice the girls jumping in. My father taught us all how to swim, even the girls. Even

Mary, that summer before he passed away. And I taught Arthur and Benjamin last summer."

Benjamin's foot slipped with a loud splash, and both children laughed.

"But they're making too much noise. And I suppose if they fall in, we'll have to take them back for a change of clothes." George beckoned, and Benjamin came running with Mary close behind.

"We can't have you splashing around scaring away all the fish. Go and do something else." He waved a hand, shooing them. "Climb a tree."

They ran off into a nearby thicket, laughing.

"Climb a tree, George?" Simon asked. "Is Fitz raising a hoyden?"

"All of the Lovelace girls climb trees. Except for one."

"Nancy."

He shook his head. "Cassandra. Too afraid of heights."

* * *

JAMES YAWNED, RUBBED HIS EYES, AND SENT NANCY A look so calculating, she couldn't believe she'd just woken him. "Why should I switch roles with you?"

Perched on the side of his bed, she ran through her options for bribery. She had pin and birthday money saved up, but she'd already promised the maid, Meg, a whole guinea for her help, and she must keep some aside for her coach fare. She could offer him five pounds—six or seven at the very most —but that money was her absolute emergency fund if for some reason she couldn't find Sally.

Instead of money, James might like the elegant pen set that Papa had given her, but she'd already packed it, and oh, how she'd hate to part with it.

"Think of it, James. How funny it will be to pull a fast one on everyone."

"What role was I to play that you want?"

She watched him a long moment. "Cassandra didn't tell you last night?"

"No." He grinned.

She snatched up a pillow and hit him. "Liar. She told you and so did Mama. Where did you go last night? I came to look for you."

He shrugged.

"I heard Mama warn you about sneaking out at night. How did you get past the footman at the end of the passage?"

"He fell asleep. You won't tell, will you? I'll deny it if you do."

"Mama ought to lock you in your bedchamber."

"She threatened to do that."

"Where do you go... Never mind. If I knew, I'd have to tell Fitz."

Likely her brother was meeting up with some village boys to drink ale and cast dice. Fitz probably already knew and was tolerating it because it was the sort of stunt he himself had pulled when he was James's age.

She stood up from the low bed—not much more than a cot, really—and walked to the narrow window under the eaves. The morning breeze brought in fresh air but it still didn't chase out the stuffiness. Outside, it was a straight drop to the ground, and an escapee would be visible from the stables.

It was a step up from sleeping with the babies in the crowded nursery though. Her own room was small but well-furnished, with a narrow tester bed, bright hangings, a clothes press and dressing table as well as two windows that let in light and air. A tree next to the window provided much needed afternoon shade, and through its branches she could see out into the park.

An easy reach from the windowsill was a sturdy limb, and once or twice, she'd climbed out there herself.

"There's more to this plot," James said. "What are you up to?"

She walked to the end of the bed and crossed her arms. "Simple. Revenge."

He jumped out of bed and came to stand next to her. "On the Swilling Duke?" His eyes glinted with amusement.

She'd hooked him. Now to reel him in.

"As you know, he vomited on me in front of

everyone and then knocked me down and fell on top of me when he passed out. It was disgusting. I was a laughingstock, especially after he ran away from town without even an apology."

"But you weren't a total laughingstock. You had marriage offers, I've heard."

She shuddered. "From a fortune-hunting dunce and a lascivious old man."

"Is that it? He didn't do anything else?"

She'd never told anyone everything, but her mother knew some of it. She could tell James that much.

"He was rude to me. He brushed me aside so he could get to Miss Hazelton and her forty thousand pounds."

"How was he rude? What did he say?"

"You'll gossip."

He put one hand on his heart and held up the other so she could see his fingers weren't crossed.

She knew her brother and she didn't trust him for a moment.

"He eyed me up and down and said, 'You chit, you're a pretty enough baggage, but you're in my way.'"

Of course, there'd been much more that evening, earlier in that back corridor, but she wouldn't tell James about that kiss.

James's eyes widened and gleamed with amusement. "In a ballroom? He was that bosky?"

"Yes, but holding himself together well enough at that point to not wobble. I was mortified."

"If I'd been there, I would've had a good comeback."

"That's why I need you. I'm to be Hermia to his Lysander tonight. I need you to play Hermia. I need your glib tongue to lash him, for he certainly deserves it. I'll never be able to think fast enough."

"You thought fast enough with that glass of wine last night."

"I'll give you five pounds."

He flapped a hand. "I won that much last night at dice."

"*Five* pounds?"

Five pounds was a veritable fortune. Oh, it was a relief though to know that he didn't need it. Five pounds would get her to Birmingham and the safety of her friend's home.

But what poor lads and working men had he swindled to win that money?

"Yes. It was great fun."

"From whom did you win the money?"

"You'll tell." He rubbed his jaw which, she observed, was still beardless. He wouldn't have to shave. "Hmm. I played Juliet at school."

He put a hand to his head. "Romeo, Romeo, wherefore art thou Romeo?" he proclaimed in a falsetto. "But I say, sister, swapping roles? I'm more suited to playing Puck. I'm very good at pranks."

"Yes. And this will be the greatest prank of all. We'll make him suffer. Only but think, James, of the humiliation for a proud man like Simon, a duke, when he discovers he's been matched up with a *boy* in a dress. Fitz says the duke is out fishing, hoping to run into me so he can apologize. He won't find me this morning, and if he tries to apologize tonight at the party, he'll learn that he's been groveling to *you* instead of *me*. He'll be furious that we tricked him. And meanwhile, I have other pranks in mind. I've been up half the night planning. I want to enlist Edward, Arthur, Mary, and Benjamin to help as well."

James grinned. "Mary would make a devilish fairy. But Meg and the nursery maid won't let them out of their sight."

Meg had served as nursery maid since she was fourteen. She'd come to London to work as Nancy's maid for the Season and become engaged to one of the London grooms.

"Meg will help. She was with me in London, remember, and she's leaving service soon to get married. Plus, I've bribed her."

"Impressive." His eyes glowed. "Pranks and hijinks—Mama warned me, but Cass... she might not approve, though what fun it might be watching her interrupt Saulsfield's card game with hysterics. Fitz and Mother will blame me though."

"I'll tell them I made you and the others do it."

"You'll fall on your sword? Then we'll both be punished, but they won't lock *you* in your room." He smiled his devious smile. "Unless you happen to be sleeping here in *mine*." He stuck out his hand. "Swap bedchambers as payment? Just until I return to school?"

She looked around the gloomy closet of a chamber and thought of her bright, airy room.

Which she was planning to run away from anyway.

"You have an excellent tree by your window. It's the price of revenge," he said, grinning.

She eyed her brother. They shared the same coloring and height. He'd wear a wig and a mask, and her small womanly curves were easily achieved with a bit of padding and a fichu in that ridiculous gown.

"All right." She shook his hand. "I have some ideas."

"As do I. My time at school hasn't all been wasted on Latin and Greek. Plus, I've made a friend of the apothecary's apprentice. Now." James picked up a wrinkled pair of trousers. "I'm starving. While I'm dressing, fetch a breakfast tray and I'll be in my new bedchamber waiting."

CHAPTER FOUR

*S*imon eyed the group of early arrivals seated around the table for luncheon.

Miss Marietta Hazelton and her elderly chaperone had arrived around noon, as had Cassandra's husband, Saulsfield.

Sir Percy Nacton had also appeared early, though he was a near enough neighbor that he wasn't spending the night. He might have waited to impose himself on the company.

A cold collation had been laid for luncheon, the servants being busy elsewhere preparing for the evening's events. Nancy and her brother James were missing, as were the younger children, who must be taking their meal in the nursery.

Lucky children. Simon would have appreciated being elsewhere, or at least having the nursery brigade's antics distracting the cloying Miss Hazelton.

As the meal ended, Cassandra announced a short meeting about the evening's festivities. She fussed about the absence of Nancy and James until Fitz told her to pack it in and get on with what she really wanted to say.

While Cassandra assigned roles—they would merely present a Midsummer Night's Dream tableau for the rest of the guests at the midnight unmasking, not act out the entire play, there being no time for rehearsals—Miss Hazelton sent Simon coy looks from the seat she'd taken next to him. Dark-haired and blue-eyed, she was a tolerable looking girl with good teeth and a fine bosom on display. He didn't truly remember her, but apparently, he'd danced with her twice at Lady Chilcombe's ball before passing out while leading her into supper.

"Sir Percy," Cassandra said, "you're to be Demetrius."

Miss Hazelton reached for her teacup and brushed Simon's hand with a twittering laugh of faux embarrassment.

Ignoring her, he bit back a smile, reminded of last night's wine spilling. Where was that challenging minx?

"And Miss Hazelton, you'll be Helena. Your grace will take the role of Lysander, and Nancy will be Hermia, if I can find her."

Miss Hazelton exclaimed that she'd be willing to take Hermia's role. But with a smile directed at Simon, Fitz's mother, Lady Neda Loughton, said amiably that there was no need, as Nancy knew the plans for the party and her role, and was busy in the garden where servants were setting up.

Simon eyed the doorway wondering how quickly he could escape. Dukes were expected to be polite, yet they were also free to be rude, weren't they?

A flash of white skirts and blonde hair moved past the door clutching a basket, and he resolved to do just what he wished.

"Do excuse me." He rose from the table, determined to shake himself free of the heiress's attentions. "I must go and find my partner for the evening."

"I'll come along," Percy called from his end of the table.

"No, you will not," Simon said.

"You must all stay," Cassandra called.

Simon had already reached the door and he continued out of it, ignoring the clamor.

Sometimes it was good to be a duke.

The figure in white slipped through a baize door at the end of the passage. He hurried to catch up.

* * *

NANCY HEARD THE DOOR CLOSE SOFTLY BEHIND HER, then heard it open again, the footsteps growing louder. She hastily rearranged the cloth covering her basket and quickened her steps.

There was much to do, and she'd spent an inordinate amount of time getting to the folly and back.

"Nancy."

Her heart stuttered, recognizing the voice. The Swilling Duke touched her elbow.

She stayed perfectly still then made the tiniest of curtsies to the empty space next to him.

"A moment of your time," he said smoothly.

He wouldn't be nervous of course. Not like her. Of course not, the arrogant toad. A touch, a command in that rich baritone voice, and one must fall at his feet and obey.

She mustered her anger and courage. "What is it?

"Will you not look at me?"

When she locked in her heels, he moved in front of her, presenting her with an eyeful of the white linen of his neckcloth. The touch of his hand cradling her jaw sent a wild flurry of heat through her. When she lifted her gaze, she found him studying her, his emotions—if he had any—veiled.

Anger pounded through her. Of course, he had no emotions. All those years, she'd remembered Simon as a kind young man, but in truth, he was heartless.

She must answer in kind.

"I'm busy," she said, infusing her tone with boredom.

He blinked as if coming out of a trance.

"Of course—the party. To be expected."

So condescending of you.

"However..." his thumb moved a fraction and her nerves leaped. "Cassandra was looking for you. You're to play Hermia to my Lysander. She's going over the plan for the evening's tableau."

A *tableau*? Cassandra was relishing her power. She'd always been jealous of Nancy's abilities to organize a family dramatic presentation. Well, so be it.

"To take place just before the unmasking, she said."

By then, Nancy would have made her escape to the folly where her valise was waiting. "And?"

He blinked again, and she caught a twinkle of humor. She shifted her basket and lifted his hand away, but he quickly twisted his wrist and captured her hand in a warm, dry grasp that had butterflies chasing up her arm, across her shoulders, and down her spine.

"Please," he said. "Just listen. I'm sorry. I apologize for my atrocious behavior at Lady Chilcombe's ball. It was abominable of me to... to insult you that way. Will you forgive me?"

Eyes still twinkling, he'd stumbled over his

abominableness. Not because he thought what he did was so terrible, but because Nancy was too insignificant, too unimportant for him to have remembered the details. And because anyway, he was a duke and nothing he did was so awful that it couldn't be forgiven.

"In what way did you insult me?" she asked.

The twinkle disappeared and he transformed into a naughty schoolboy caught out in mischief. "I'm told that I cast up my accounts, ruining your gown, and then I knocked you down and fell on you when I, er, collapsed."

"You remember nothing else?"

He frowned and squeezed his eyes shut a moment. Seeking her sympathy, probably, *poor confused duke*.

"Will you not tell me? I was so thoroughly foxed that the night is a blur."

"Thoroughly foxed, yet you managed to dance several dances."

His eyes lit. "Was that it? I didn't ask you to dance?" He squeezed her hand. "I'll make it up to you tonight. We'll dance every dance together, if you wish."

She scoffed. To dance every dance together would be a declaration of pending nuptials, and he would know that.

Though if it was James who partnered him through the evening, and then was revealed at the unmasking, how could anyone expect her and Simon to marry?

No... no. She would not dance with Simon, nor would James in his Hermia disguise. Simon didn't deserve the courtesy.

"Please forgive me, Nancy."

Though he was clear-eyed today and steadier on his feet, he had the same confident male swagger he'd had the night of the ball. He'd had that swagger all his life, really, as long as she'd known him. What a little fool she'd been to follow him around like a puppy and spin dreams of romance.

Like her brothers, he'd shooed her away and ignored her often enough. That night at Lady Chilcombe's, she'd been an idiot to think he'd be any different now, that he'd be kind because it was her first ball, and she was nervous. She'd been an idiot to imagine he'd even know who she was.

The memory of that night swept over her, and his face blurred.

That kiss. And then the slap on her bottom. Mother had forced her to leave the retiring room and dance with an old friend of her father's.

After that, she'd been separated from Mother on the edge of the dance floor when a man bumped into her again. She'd looked up into Simon's blurry eyes. Though her tongue twisted into angry knots, she finally managed to speak.

"*Your grace. You don't remember me. I'm George's sister.*"

"*Still here, little bird? Every Covent Garden dove has a brother named George. Told you, you shouldn't be here. They'll toss you out on your shapely arse. You're a pretty enough baggage, but you're in my way.*" He wagged a finger. "*Heiresses waiting for me over there.*"

She shook off the nightmarish memory and drew in a tight breath. "You're a duke. You don't need my forgiveness."

He opened his mouth to reply, but she spoke first.

"Nor shall you have it," she said mustering a calm tone. "Nor will I grant you a dance. Ever."

His eyes flashed and color rose in his firm jaws and into his cheeks.

She tugged her hand away, jarring her basket, and the cloth slipped, spilling the shriveled roses she'd collected from the folly rose garden.

When she bent to retrieve them, her head bumped something hard.

"*Fustian,*" she said rubbing her forehead. Simon was grinning, his hand at his jaw.

"I'm sorry. Allow me." He took the basket from her and began scooping flowers into it. "That was clumsy of me, and I *am* sorry. Though I'll probably be concussed again from bonking against your hard head. And don't tell me I'm a duke and I don't need your forgiveness. Apparently, I'm a gauche, rude, ill-mannered duke, but I've known you since you were a brat in the nursery, so I'll keep asking."

She huffed out a breath. "You... you *oaf*. Give me that."

"An oaf, am I?"

His amused voice spiked her anger.

"Yes. An arrogant, pompous, spoiled oaf." She grabbed the basket, pricked her finger on an errant thorn, and winced.

"Serves you right. What are those shriveled flowers for?"

She had wanted to use something else, but James said the dried rose hips would be more effective.

"For the party," she said. "You'll see."

She hurried down the stairs to the kitchens. She had more items to retrieve from the larder and still room.

When she reached the bottom landing, she couldn't help herself; she glanced back. He was still there, watching her, a thoughtful look on his face.

A SHORT WHILE LATER, NANCY MET JAMES IN HER room, having sent Meg off to the attics with the younger children to search the trunks for costumes.

Puck's costume lay on the bed next to the hideous bodice and skirt that would be Hermia's. Cassandra had found a simple tunic, smock, and pair of trousers for Puck, and she'd attached tiny horns to a hat. The trousers wouldn't go over Nancy's hips, but Meg would fetch a bigger pair for her from among the spare clothing they'd kept for her brothers.

James rummaged through the contents of the basket, crowing, "You did well, Nancy. We'll make a hoyden of you yet. These rose hips are perfect. You'll need work gloves and your pen knife and a steaming cup of tea. Quickly though, so we may prepare them in time."

He pulled out the mortar and pestle and a small jar of white peppercorns.

While he went to work making sneezing powder, she spread a handkerchief on her dressing table and began pulling shriveled petals from the rose hips. "There wasn't much syrup of ipecac left."

"A wee bit will do the trick. I've borrowed a dropper from the apothecary." He smiled. "And something else, if we dare. I've obtained a rare bit of Spanish fly."

Blood rushed to her face. She oughtn't to know what Spanish fly was and what it was used for, but her friend Sally and some of the other girls had shared the secrets in whispered late-night discussions after their candles had been extinguished.

"No, James."

"Nothing to worry about, it's only the tiniest bit.

I'll put a pinch in his drink. Imagine his frustration when he—"

"*No, James.*" She'd heard tales of what went on at masquerades in town. Plus, Spanish fly in the wrong dosage could be poisonous. "That's a step too far. I say no to that one, for Mama's sake."

He laughed, and then sneezed. "Very well. I also have some extract of sweet flag."

"What is that?"

"It's said to have a milder effect than the Spanish fly. Used by the ancients to ensure the happiness of their wi—"

"Stop. Just stop."

Perhaps it had been a mistake to enlist James's help. She was losing control. "There will be no aphrodisiacs tonight."

What she wanted was quite the opposite.

"Think of it, though, Nancy." James's eyes twinkled mischievously. "The Swilling Duke aching for who he thinks is you, while I, pretending to be you, continue to rebuff him."

"It's just as likely that, after you pretending to be me and rebuffing him, he'll direct that aching at someone else, such as Miss Hazelton."

James raised an eyebrow. "And you would mind that?"

The thought brought a spurt of hot jealousy and an ache to her heart. Simon had been no more than kind to her younger self. She had no claim on him, and at Lady Chilcombe's he'd made it clear he was well acquainted with the women of the demimonde. Perhaps he was one of those men who were incapable of truly caring for any one woman. The scandal sheets were filled with the antics and affairs of cheating husbands and equally unfaithful wives. What a horrible way to live out one's marriage.

"Of course not. She's welcome to him."

Nevertheless, she'd make sure James couldn't get his hand on the aphrodisiacs during the party.

The door opened and the children piled in, Meg following with a mound of garments.

"Oh miss," she said, "your mother is on the stairs. I fear she's coming this way."

"What's going on in here?" Lady Neda Loughton opened the door without knocking and stepped into the room.

Nancy hurried to greet her. "Mama, come join us. James, let Mama have that chair."

James rose from the slipper chair where he was lounging, but their mother waved him back and tousled Mary's curls as the little girl collided with her leg.

"We're having a tea party, Grandmama," Mary said. "You must join us."

Nancy saw the way her mother surveyed the

room. Her gaze stopped on the dressing table and the partially open drawer where they'd hurriedly stored their *projects*, and on the bed, where the boys, Arthur, Benjamin, and Edward had been reclining before jumping up at her entry.

"Yes, Mama," Nancy said. "Meg is going down now to fetch a tray."

Meg turned from the clothes press where she'd just shoved in costumes and dipped a curtsey.

"Fetch an extra cup will you, Meg?" Nancy said. "Edward, please go along and help her."

"I'll go as well," Arthur said.

Benjamin scooted out after them.

"Imagine, Mama," James said, "my sister, brother, niece, and step-nephews wish to spend time visiting with me. I'm honored."

Mother's look was quizzical. "Well, I am glad to hear it."

She didn't look glad. She looked suspicious.

"Grandmama." Mary tugged at Mother's hand and turned her great blue eyes up to her, batting her lashes. "May we go to the party tonight? I so want to see the costumes and fairy lights."

Mother's lips quirked as she stroked the little girl's golden curls. Mary, like her grandmother and all the Lovelace offspring except George, was fair-haired.

"Will you be good, Mary?" Mother asked.

"Yes." Mary nodded solemnly. "Oh, yes."

"And what of you, James and Nancy?"

Nancy's breath tightened. *She knew. Mother always knew.* "Of course," she said.

James held up his hands. "No crossed fingers, Mama. We just want to have fun."

"And that," Mother said, "is what I'm afraid of. Do think of your sister Cassandra's feelings and the Lovelace family name, and make sure your pranks are not too outrageous." She leaned down and hugged Mary. "I shall leave you to your tea party."

When the door closed on her, James grinned.

"She didn't say I couldn't go to the party," Mary said, clapping her hands.

"She knows," Nancy said.

"She only suspects." James jumped up and went to the dressing table. "Back to work, Puck. We have pranks to prepare."

Nancy had just finished scraping the rose hips when Meg and the boys returned with a steaming pot and a tray of cakes.

"I'm sorry I took so long," Meg said. "Miss Cassandra waylaid me to deliver the costumes for his grace and Sir Percy to his grace's bedchamber." She wrinkled her nose. "Sir Percy was the only one there, and I'd like to have smacked him the way he flirted with me."

James frowned. "They're sharing a bedchamber?"

"It's only for the dressing up," Meg said. "Sir Percy isn't staying the night."

"Two pompous prigs together," Nancy murmured.

"No, don't you see, Nancy? This complicates matters."

She shared a look with her brother and the maid. The plan had been to intercept Simon's costume before delivery and put the itching powder into it. But with Cassandra's interference, and with two men occupying the bedroom, it would be that much more difficult.

"We'll move Sir Percy somewhere else," James said.

"There's no other room free... Wait, I know." Nancy grinned. "We'll move him to your bedchamber. We'll send a footman. He doesn't have to know it's your room, we'll just say we moved one of the family members because the duke wished to have his privacy." She rubbed her hands together. "Then we just need to find a way to get the duke out of his room so Meg... or you, can add the itching powder."

"We'll need at least another hour," James said. "And as to that... I know how we can bring it about."

CHAPTER FIVE

"Your grace, what do you think of our preparations?" Fitz's wife, Mel, had appeared at his elbow.

Simon had wandered out to the gardens hoping to find Nancy, guessing that she'd come that way after her visit to the kitchens. She was nowhere to be seen, but footmen, maids, even grooms, hustled about under the direction of the Loughton Manor butler, setting up tables and chairs and a great canopy.

It looked like a devil of a thing to arrange, definitely the sort of thing one left to a wife. "Impressive. Will it be a large party?"

"Not so large. Two of Fitz's brothers and two of his sisters and their families aren't able to attend. But the local gentry will be here with their older sons and daughters. This won't be a London masquerade."

"I've never attended a London masquerade." At least not one hosted by polite society. In his much younger days, when he was in England between military assignments, he'd gone with a friend to a party hosted by the demimonde.

"No?" She laughed. "Not a *ton* one, you mean. Fitz told me about the other sort."

He looked at her, and his astonishment must have shown on his face.

"You and I have met before, your grace, though I'm sure you don't remember, at the winter camp in Frenada. My father was Major Parker."

He'd spent much of that winter chasing a local girl with hair and eyes as dark as this Lady Loughton's.

"Of course, you wouldn't remember," she said. "My mother and I returned to England soon after."

"You didn't follow the drum after that?"

"Oh yes. Before and after, when my mother was... You may have heard of my mother, Lady Starling."

"Ah." What was one to say? Lady Starling had provided a great deal of fodder for the gossips and the scandal sheets.

"Now," she took his arm, "I've heard that Miss Hazelton is looking for you. I can help you seek her out, or I can take you to Fitz's study where he's hiding from Cassandra."

"I was hoping to find Nancy. We had a bit of a…" Not a row. It hadn't come to that. "I bumped into her, and we, er, had words."

She eyed him speculatively. "Do you know, of all of Fitz's siblings, Nancy is the very dearest to me. I haven't seen her all morning."

Nancy certainly was dear if the lady was granting her a dowry from her sizeable fortune. But there'd been a hint of a warning in that tone.

"Then, by all means, I'll take refuge in Fitz's study, if you please."

* * *

MEL LEFT HIM AT THE STUDY DOOR. IT WAS GEORGE he found behind the desk working, while Fitz lounged in another chair. Simon had just seated himself when the dowager Lady Loughton arrived.

It was hard to believe the petite, still-attractive lady had borne such tall strapping sons, or indeed, so many healthy children. She'd raised, and was still raising, four daughters and six sons, yet there was nothing careworn about her.

"Mama," George said, and all three men stood. "How go the plans for the party?"

"A bit chaotic at present, but all shall go well, and Cassandra shall have a triumph." Her lips quirked.

"Perhaps the next big event she'll want to host at her own estate. Now, before you take your seat again, your grace, I'd like a few moments of your time."

Her expression was unreadable.

George and Fitz shared amused glances.

He recalled in his many school holiday visits to Loughton Manor that he'd never heard Lady Loughton raise her voice, unlike his own mother, who'd alternated between screaming and hysterical tears to get her way.

Lady Loughton had been at Lady Chilcombe's ball. She'd witnessed his reprehensible conduct. He was in for her quiet kind of discipline.

He, a grown man, a full foot taller, and more importantly a duke.

"Yes, of course, my lady."

* * *

SIMON FOLLOWED LADY NEDA LOUGHTON INTO HER private sitting room and took the chair she directed him to.

Back straight, hands folded in her lap, she began whatever sort of discussion this was to be. "I recall fondly your visits here when you were younger, your grace."

"Will you not call me Simon?"

She shook her head. "We must get used to your new life. It's a grand title you've inherited, and a particular sort of life you'll be expected to lead. Great responsibilities to the Crown and those who depend upon you."

He nodded. "I confess, despite my initial elation, it has weighed on me."

"I'm happy to hear you're taking your new role seriously. Now, I must ask you, what are your intentions toward my Nancy?"

Ah. It was to be that sort of a talk.

His future flashed before him: estates to manage, necessary entertainments to arrange, speeches and votes in Lords. Visiting his estates had been damned lonely, each line of the ledgers hammering him more into a future he'd never imagined—never truly hankered after. It wouldn't be the sort of future he'd dreamed of—a settled home like Loughton Manor, a sprawling family like the Lovelaces had.

Nor would it be the sort of life he'd expected: a career in the army, traveling the world, ending his days in some far-flung battle, or if he was lucky, coming back to England and retiring. He'd thought that, perhaps, when he was too old to gad about bedding widows, he'd find some comfortable lady to marry.

Now, he'd need a *son* by a *wife*. Society expected her to be well-bred. His estates needed someone wealthy.

He'd tossed and turned all night after his conversation with George and Fitz, seeing the future as more than just a vague dreaded outline of bedding a wife until he had an heir and a spare, and then going their separate ways. He'd thought of Nancy; Nancy managing dinners and parties; Nancy organizing the servants at all their estates; Nancy, chasing away the loneliness of country evenings.

Nancy in his bed, her golden hair spilling across the pillows, her curves filling his hands.

He shook himself out of his woolgathering to find Lady Loughton watching him.

Nancy must have learned much from the lady before him who'd been so good to his orphaned self. She and Nancy were, he suspected, much alike in disposition and character—kind, gentle, abiding, and it seemed Nancy had at least some of her mother's strength. Depths of stubbornness, George had called it.

He mustered his courage. "I wish to court her. And if she will have me, marry her."

"Yes. My sons have told me as much."

He nodded, uncertain what to say. Her tone was kind, her gaze implacable.

"Why, your grace?" she asked, breaking the silence. "Why Nancy? Because I must say in all honesty, as a duke, you might find a substantial dowry with a lady such as Miss Hazelton, and perhaps she'll be willing to endure a society marriage where, after the succession is ensured, you both go your separate ways. My daughter deserves better than that."

He could do nothing about the rush of heat to his cheeks but he held his hands still to keep them from clenching. This was the sort of declaration he'd expect from Fitz or George.

Lady Loughton leaned closer. "The words must be said, your grace. What does a parent want for his or her child's marriage? A stable home, a comfortable income, healthy children. And more. My daughter deserves to be loved. She deserves to be treated well. It is my wish that she find a husband, a man of honor, who will fulfill both of those requirements, as well as the practical ones. So," tilting her head, she studied him. "Tell me why you wish to court her."

The kindly tone was disarming, and he damped down the urge to squirm. Why hadn't George and Fitz asked these questions? Why leave it to their mother?

He thought of their humorous glances earlier in the study. They hadn't asked because they knew their mother would, and because it was far more daunting speaking with *her*. Being a woman, she would think about things like love. But also being a woman of strong character, she'd care about *his* character more than his title.

"She's beautiful," he said.

And drat, that was the superficiality he ought to

avoid. He cleared his throat. "Of course there's that, but I remember her as a child. She was gentle, and serious, and as I recall, though she'd follow us around, she'd leave when her brothers sent her away."

Unless Cassandra was leading them into mischief.

"You're saying she was biddable."

"Er, I suppose." Did he want a biddable wife? "George said it was because she, er, had a tendre for me."

"Biddable," Lady Loughton, said thoughtfully. "Yes, she was, but not without spirit. And what she felt for you was mere calf love. Did you return her affections?"

He drew in a breath, remembering. He wouldn't lie to this lady. "Well, I liked her of course, but in truth, I found it a bit annoying."

She nodded, as if that had been the correct answer.

"What role does her new dowry play in your wooing?"

His breath whooshed. He ought to have expected that question. What to answer?

"No role." He swiped at his jaw. "No, I suppose that's not entirely true. I've had a tour of the ducal properties, and though I believe I can bring things into order in a few years..." Perhaps twenty or thirty. "An influx of money would help greatly."

Lady Loughton gazed at the cold fireplace. "I didn't agree with Mel increasing Nancy's dowry. My dear husband arranged dowries for our four girls. Not substantial, perhaps, but none of them would go into marriage penniless. Nancy might have found a clergyman or a member of the local gentry, someone who would appreciate her intelligence and quiet good humor. She had offers of marriage in the spring, you know, but now, it will be worse. Every handsome, charming man with pockets to let will flock to her."

She gave him a steely eyed look. He'd been called handsome before he was called the Duke of Swillingstone, he'd charmed a few women into his bed, and he'd been more or less pockets to let his whole life.

"However, Mel explained to me that the money she is providing will be in a trust. The terms of access will be negotiated in any marriage settlement, but in effect, Nancy's husband will not have much control. My girl will not fall prey to a fortune hunter. Did my sons tell you that?"

"No." His spirits lifted. "And it doesn't matter, my lady. In truth, I've found the notion of marrying for money distasteful."

"Ah. You've come around to that opinion? You didn't seem to feel that way when you were in London dancing with heiresses."

He felt his cheeks heating again.

"Well then, you may court her, your grace, but it will take more than your handsome face and your title to rekindle that childish tendre and win her heart."

"I can see that. I had something of a row with her this morning. She's unwilling to forgive me. I know I was abominable at that ball, but I fear there must be more than the, er, unfortunate scene in the supper room. Will you not tell me everything?"

"I will tell you that Nancy hugged the walls of every ball we attended after that. She is, as you noted, disposed to be gentle and serious and occasionally a bit socially awkward. She's not boisterous, and even when she was organizing the family for pageants and plays, she never truly needed to be the center of attention. The Season can be daunting for such girls. At her first London ball, her confidence was shattered—by you. I made her attend parties and routs and musicales. She went, as I required, and though she joined the ranks of wallflowers, her deepest friendships are still with her sisters."

"My lady, *please* tell me—I intend to make this up to her—but I must know. Besides the unfortunate scene at the supper room, what else did I do?"

"You must ask her." She shifted in her chair and smoothed her skirts. "And let me remind you that others have an interest in courting her. Your title won't make you an easy winner."

His fingers threatened to curl into fists. Percy Nacton was surely one of those eager admirers.

"And I hope your courtship has nothing to do with that masculine need to win at all costs. I hope the Simon Clayding I knew is better than that."

Feeling as though he ought to slink out with his tail tucked between his legs, he bowed over the dowager's hand and made his way to his bedchamber.

He found Nacton stretched out on the sofa there, yawning.

"Good of you to let me dress here tonight," Percy said.

It just needed this. "I see you've made yourself comfortable, Percy."

"It's Sir Percy now, i'n't, your grace? Who would have thought when we were trudging through the Peninsula that we'd both have a title someday. Though you won the greater prize."

"An accident of birth." Simon shed his coats and went to the washstand, splashing the tepid water on his face. He'd need to shave again before the evening festivities.

"I'll need your man's help," Percy said.

"I didn't bring my valet." Simon walked to the window and pushed the sash higher. They'd had two days of sunny, dry weather and the late June air was stifling.

"No?"

The late duke's valet had dutifully traveled with Simon to all his estates and proved useful enough to earn a bit of a holiday. "No. I've sent him on to London where he's busy organizing my wardrobe. One of the footmen can help you."

"Good. Want to look my best tonight." Percy stood, lifted a garment from the back of a chair, and carried it over. "My costume," he said with a grin.

The long vest and frilly shirt must have been the height of fashion a century earlier.

"You'll look quite the peacock," Simon said.

"I hope so. Two heiresses here tonight. I hear Miss Nancy will bring even more to a marriage than Miss Hazelton. And unless she's lost her memory, I've got a leg up on you with Miss Nancy."

Blood surged into Simon's hands as jealousy flooded him. Percy was a fit, well-built man, an inch taller than himself. He was also one of those handsome, sweet-talking men with pockets to let that Lady Neda Loughton mentioned.

Like himself. Except that *he* knew Nancy. And cared for her.

"Your costume is over there. A maid brought them, a pretty little thing named Meg."

Simon sent Percy a look, and he held up his hands.

"No. Didn't touch her," he said. "Don't want to ruin my reputation at Loughton Manor, now do I?"

"There are no camp señoritas or soldiers' wives here. Keep that in mind."

"I'll do that, your grace." A gleam of amusement lit the other man's eyes. "And no Covent Garden doves about here either. Though I recall you were able to resist the charms of that fair-haired whore we met on Lady Chilcombe's square."

Simon winced, an unsettling feeling roiling through him. Percy oughtn't to be sitting in Loughton Manor talking about prostitutes.

Before he could craft a reply that would get through the oaf's thick head, a footman arrived to fetch Percy to another bedchamber the Lovelaces had found for him, and to deliver a note to Simon.

"Well then, I'll see you later, your grace." Percy shrugged into the coats he'd tossed aside while the footman gathered up his costume.

When the door closed, Simon unfolded the paper, and his heart began to race.

If you wish to see Nancy alone, you will find her in the music room. I trust you still remember where that is.

The scrawled masculine hand must be Fitz's or George's.

He rubbed his face. Shaving could wait. If Nancy was there, he wanted another chance to speak with her alone before this fiasco of a masquerade could commence.

* * *

NANCY HURRIED DOWN THE STAIRS, TRYING NOT TO bump the balusters with the awkward panniers of the century-old gown. The low neckline revealed far too much and ought to be covered, but James had pushed her out the door before she could find a fichu.

And, gad, but she reeked of lavender. Cassandra had seen all the clothing she'd chosen for costumes aired out, but despite that, the scent they were packed in would linger for days. Even the Swilling Duke would smell like the housekeeper's stored linen.

Wrestling her nerves into a calm demeanor, she tiptoed through the hall. The servants were busy in the kitchen or outside. Everyone else was upstairs preparing for the ball.

She couldn't help thinking this was a very bad idea. Oh, but they needed to get the duke out of his bedchamber, and the only lure sure to draw him out was the chance to speak with her.

James had insisted it would work to their advantage to have the Swilling Duke see her in the Hermia costume because then, later, in the twinkling light of the garden, he wouldn't question the shadowy figure of James playing the part.

Or so James had declared. Rascally James. That business of the Spanish fly... She had no wish to harm the duke with some poisonous herb. That bit of mischief would go straight into the pocket of Puck's tunic, once she'd changed into it.

Not for the first time, she wondered if she could truly trust her little brother. However, though she knew her lines well for the evening, she couldn't carry out this prank without her brother's deviously clever mind. She needed all the older boys, really, including the more sober Arthur. She'd endured a coaching session by the three of them, who all claimed experience of practical jokes at school.

As long as the addlepated boys didn't go too far.

Now, James required access to the duke's room for at least a quarter hour, perhaps longer if Mother was roaming the corridors.

Breathing a sigh of relief, she saw that the drawing room adjoining the music room was deserted, and she wouldn't have to deal with her family, or worse, Sir Percy or Miss Hazelton.

Her heart quickened again when she saw the music room door ajar.

Memories flooded her. Years ago, Simon had stood in that doorway dressed in his regimentals, handsome beyond belief, listening as she'd stumbled over a piece for her family, one she'd usually played flawlessly when he wasn't around. On leave from his unit, he'd come to spend that early Easter at Loughton Manor.

He'd clapped dutifully and complimented her on her playing, and then he'd gone off with George to the billiards room. The next morning, he was gone, called back to duty because of Bonapart's escape from Elba. That he'd almost departed without a goodbye had left her heartbroken.

She set her hand to the doorknob and gathered her courage. Best to tear open the old wounds as well as the newer ones so she'd be able to play her part tonight.

Squaring her shoulders, she bumped through the doorway and then sailed for the shelf near the harp where the music was stored.

Halfway to her destination she knew with certainty he was here. Not close enough for his scent to reach her over all the stale lavender, not yet, but the dark shape framed in the late afternoon light was Simon.

CHAPTER SIX

"*N*ancy?" He turned away from the window where he'd been gazing out over the side lawns. Still attired in the coats he'd worn earlier, he'd loosened his neckcloth, and his curls were in their usual disarray.

He'd not donned his costume yet. That was good. That was why she was here—not to fetch sheet music, not to meet with him secretly, not to feel goosebumps traveling up and down her back. She was here to play a part, while James put the final touches to Simon's costume.

She struck a regal pose and looked down her nose at him. "What are you doing here, your grace?"

Eyes sparkling, he moved closer, looking her up and down, hesitating over her bosom. "Is *that* your costume?" A smile hovered on his lips. "It's… it's…"

"Hideous. Feel free to say it."

"No. Never. Anything *you* wear is bound to be ravishing."

What fustian. "Ah, then, you'll like the wig that goes with this. One could hide a whole family of dormice in it."

She swept past him bumping him with her pannier. "Beg pardon," she said, but when she tried to move on, he captured her elbow.

"What are you looking for? Let me fetch it before you knock over the harp with your skirts."

Grrr. She rarely forgot her lines, but she hadn't planned an answer to that question.

Improvise. "A reel, and I can't remember the name, but I'll know it when I see it."

"I'll just grab a stack of music sheets, shall I? Can you sit down in those hoops? Here." He led her to the pianoforte bench.

"Oh, go away, and I'll find it myself more quickly."

He ignored her and she sighed, pacing while he collected music sheets, watching the descent of the late afternoon sun. Upstairs, James was carrying out the mission in the duke's bedchamber, while the other boys were fashioning wings for Mary, donkey ears for both Anthony and Edward, and a headpiece with horns for Benjamin.

How much time did James need? There was no clock in the music room, so she strained her ears to hear the mantel clock in the nearby drawing room strike the quarter hour.

"Ah. This one."

The Swilling Duke returned with one music sheet and handed it to her.

Her breath quickened. *Sheep May Safely Graze.* "This is not a reel. It's Bach."

"No? *Sheep may safely graze and pasture, in a watchful shepherd's sight.* It's the piece I hummed all the way to Brussels. You played it for us when I was here at Easter in 1815. Will you play it again now for me?"

Her heart did a flip, warmth coursing through her. *He remembered. He'd hummed it all the way to Brussels.*

That Easter, they'd learned that Napoleon had escaped from Elba and was gathering an army to confront his enemies. Men who'd gone home on leave after so many years of fighting were called back. Simon was one of them.

She'd always thought he was the best of her brothers' friends, but during that visit she'd fallen head over ears in love with him, as only a silly goose would do. From the day he'd departed, she'd prayed long and hard for his safety. Oh, how her nerves had trembled reading the casualty lists, until the news finally arrived that he'd survived.

When he'd never returned to Loughton Manor for a visit, she'd tucked away her disappointment and hoped that he'd stay single and wait for her. And then continued to pray for his safety in the many places where he went on to serve.

It hadn't seemed foolish then. What a widgeon she'd been.

"That piece always reminded me of, well, home. I was impressed at how well you played for one so young. You were... only ten, was it?"

She nodded.

"So will you play it again now? For me?"

Now? "No." The music might draw in another guest or worse, her mother. "Not now."

The piece reminded him of home—but what did that mean? Loughton Manor? England? According to George, Simon had passed through England a few times during the last nine years, but he'd never returned to Loughton Manor.

She shook her head, determined she'd not fall for his charms. Oh, his kiss at Lady Chilcombe's ball had been ravishing, but the callous words, the slap on the bottom...

"Will you play it for the party tonight?"

"Certainly not. I came to f-fetch..." Hades, she'd have to do better than this. She took in a breath. "I only came to fetch some... some country dances."

"Let's find some German waltzes as well." He carried back a stack of music and led her into the drawing room where he took her hand and seated her on a sofa, plopping the music sheets on the low table before them.

He sat down next to her, or rather next to her pannier. She glanced at the clock. The minute hand had barely moved.

"Here," he said, taking half of the stack and settling it into her lap. His hand lingered on hers for a long moment, stopping her breath, sending her heart racing and her pulse pounding.

"Do you have them?" he asked innocently. "I don't want them to slide off. I might bump heads with you again."

The smile that followed was brash, boyish, charming—oh, so much that, and it made her heart tumble.

But she knew it was false. The clever, clever Swilling Duke was simply trying to woo her into forgiving him.

A wave of sadness swept over her. He didn't truly care for her, not a bit; he only wanted to stay on good terms with his best friend's family. A *chit* he'd called her at Lady Chilcombe's ball—the least of his insults—and he'd been right about that. She'd been young and silly to think that he'd have any interest in her for herself.

He'd remembered the Bach piece but so what? It had merely stuck in his mind, a last memory of his friend's peaceful home, because of the fierce battle at Waterloo that followed.

Out of the corner of her eye she saw him pick up the rest of the music sheets and look through them.

"Ah, here's one," he said. "Wilson's Waltz suite."

She'd watched him dance that waltz with Miss Hazelton at Lady Chilcombe's ball after her mother had fetched her back from the lady's retiring room for the third time that night.

"I'll give it to the musicians. Will you not dance it with me tonight, Nancy?"

"Do you not think, your grace, that Miss Hazelton will want to dance it with you again?"

He blinked.

"No," he said. "If I've ever danced with her, I've completely forgotten it. I want to dance it with you."

How shallow men could be. How little attention they paid to a lady's feelings.

Not that she felt any bond with Miss Hazelton. They hadn't become friends.

Surely James had completed his mission by now. She flipped through her stack and found a Playford edition of country dances so old that the pages were slipping out. "These will do."

She started to stand, but he grabbed her free hand and, wedging himself awkwardly between the table and sofa, went down on one knee.

Heart pounding, she plopped onto the sofa again, hugging the music book one-handed to her heart like a shield.

"Nancy," he said. "Would you make me the happiest of men. Would you—"

"Stop." She hissed, her breath shaky. "Go no further. I know what this is about. *Blasted* Fitz and *blasted* George have told you of that *blasted* dowry."

"No," he said. "I mean, yes, but your mother explained—"

"*My mother*? My mother as well? How could she think..." Tears pricked the corners of her eyes and clogged her throat. Mama was betraying her—she'd not indulge in any more guilty feelings about the valise she'd stowed at the folly or her escape to Birmingham in the morning.

She blinked back the tears. "My mother doesn't know what you *did*, what you *said*. Perhaps no one else saw you or heard you either. But I can't forget."

"What, Nancy? What did I do. What did I say?"

She gulped back another rush of moisture. "First... first, in the hallway when you k-kissed me. And then later, on the edge of the dance floor. Simon Clayding, you... you despicable, loathsome, vile reprobate. You... you called me a *whore*. You may go to the devil. Let me stand."

His mouth had dropped open. His suave condescension, his façade of charm, vanished, and she saw a world of shame in his eyes.

He didn't remember?

She'd worried that if he remembered what he'd

done, he would boast about it when he was in his cups again, make her even more of a laughingstock. Because what did she really know about the kind of man Simon had grown to be?

She ought to have lashed him with the truth sooner.

"I called you... Oh, Nancy." He squeezed her hand.

The charming rogue was temporarily silenced. The Swilling Duke had disappeared.

Yet he still gripped her hand and she couldn't escape, and she desperately needed to before she burst into tears.

"Nancy, I'm so... very sorry." Then he frowned, and she saw the doubt creeping in. "I'm mortified. I was... I was..."

"You don't believe me."

"I do, but—"

"Hah. Don't claim drunkenness as your defense, Swilling Duke. You were not *that* fuddled. You managed to stand up with several ladies. It was not until the supper dance that you were so potted you could no longer stand."

His brows drew together in a frown. "I... I kissed you?"

She squeezed her eyes shut, shoving down the memory. "Yes. And it was no mere peck on the cheek."

When she opened her eyes, he'd leaned closer and his gaze had darkened, sending a flood of remembered sensation, the feel of his lips, the press of his big body.

Must. Not. Think. About that.

What came after that passionate embrace was so unforgiveable it ought to have made the kiss seem loathsome. Instead, his scent, his nearness, his sheer masculinity and the memory of his lips pressed to hers, his tongue searching her mouth, were like magnets tugging her closer.

And she must not allow it.

She cleared her throat. "You told me *Percy* could pay me. Your friend, Sir Percy, I suppose? And then you *slapped* me on my *bottom* and told me to get out."

His thumb swept across the back of her hand, sending an unwelcome shiver through her.

She smacked him on the head with the Playford collection. "Let go of my hand."

His eyes widened, and she smacked him again. Pages flew everywhere.

Wrestling her hand away, she tossed the remaining music on the table and fled, battling the tears flooding her eyes.

James's time in the Swilling Duke's bedchamber was up.

* * *

SIMON CLIMBED TO HIS FEET IN A DAZE, IDLY PICKING up pages of music, restoring them to the ancient publication.

He'd kissed her, she said. And he'd almost kissed her again, today. Would have if she hadn't broken the spell.

Setting the music aside, he buried his face in his hands, trying to pull the threads of his memory now that Nancy had given him the worst of it.

He'd kissed Nancy. Not a peck on the cheek.

He had a vague impression of a woman that night at one of the parties he'd been to. Pretty, blonde, statuesque. He'd thought to himself, she'd make a plum piece to set up on the side.

His fingers worked through the scruff at his jaw. He still needed to shave. And...

The soiled dove had followed him to Lady Chilcombe's.

Only, apparently, that had been Nancy. His vision had been as fuzzy as his brain.

Shame swept through him, triggering more details. He'd cast up his accounts, yes. He'd fallen. He knew all of that from the caricature, and from the state of his stomach and the lump on his head the next day.

But earlier... Two heiresses would attend Lady Chilcombe's ball, the fellows at White's had said. He and Percy had found their way to Lady Chilcombe's square. Somehow. Had they walked?

Outside a townhouse on the square, they'd encountered two ladies and learned that the fashionable young buck who lived there, an acquaintance of Nacton, was hosting a party. Someone had shouted from the front door for them to come in and they entered together. "The dark one for me," Percy whispered, "and the blonde one for you."

Inside, they were met with bare bums, bare breasts, and impossible tangles.

Percy's friend was hosting an orgy.

Simon had a distaste for prostitutes—not even an excess of spirits could overcome that—and Percy had dreadful luck picking healthy ones.

While Percy indulged himself and the gathering degenerated further, Simon found his way to Lady Chilcombe's, arriving unfashionably early, and gratified there'd be no competition for the heiresses.

Not that he'd feared competition from Percy, not with a duchess's coronet on offer.

His hostess greeted him, and a footman directed him down a corridor to the gentleman's retiring room. Somehow, lost in a back passageway, he turned a corner and ran into a statuesque blonde girl, who called him by name.

His mouth went dry. In his fuzzy brainbox, he'd thought she was one of the doves—the blonde one—accosting him. He came away with the impression that town balls were rather shabby affairs if a lightskirt could sneak in.

He stared vacantly at the jumbled music sheets. What he'd said that night, he couldn't remember. But the rest—that kiss...

It had taken all his willpower to step back, to... Hades. He *had* turned her around and spanked her.

He buried his face in his hands again, not sure whether to laugh or to cry. That beautiful, enticing girl, that girl who could kiss with such innocence and passion, that had been Nancy.

Damn, damn, damn.

And laying hands on her? There'd been times when he'd wanted to spank the young imp when she and Cassandra had plagued the boys. But now... now he couldn't help wondering if she would ever want to play that game in bed.

Likely she'd rather take a switch to *him*.

Gad, Nancy was right; he was a despicable reprobate.

And he wanted her.

He might be a duke, but he was no gentleman. Fitz and George, if they'd known the whole story, would have arranged for pistols at dawn, with or without his apology.

He paced back to the music room and remembered the little girl at the keyboard, coloring up as she mangled a note here or there but soldiering on to the end.

He'd thought of her as a mostly sweet child; he'd never really known her. The quiet young girl who'd played music with such diligence that he'd carried the memory into battle—that girl had grown into a beautiful woman, one who had hidden depths of passion, depths he'd like to explore.

He'd been about to offer marriage, and her preemptive rejection had stunned him. Dear Lord, but he'd deserved everything she'd dished out, including the slaps.

Lady Loughton had given him a chance to court Nancy; not to win her, like some prize he was competing with Percy over. But because he cared for her. And he did.

Was it possible that she might care for him? She hadn't spurred her brothers to shoot him.

He'd cling to that hope.

Taking up the book of country dances, he left to find someone to give it to.

In the hall, he met the dowager Lady Loughton, her black mask for the evening on a stick in her hand. She wore a panniered gown like Nancy's, but it was made from a heavy dark satin and trimmed with beads.

"Your grace, you're not dressed yet. I hope Sir Percy didn't chase you out of your bedchamber. We had nowhere else to put him and since he said you had served together, we hoped you wouldn't mind.

I'd meant to tell you after our discussion, but I quite forgot."

"I didn't mind at all, my lady," he said. "Percy and I have shared quarters before. But I imagine he was happy to move to his own room."

She froze, and her head tipped a fraction. "He was moved?"

"Yes. A footman came for him."

"I see."

Her lips formed a thin line. She looked very much like one of his commanders before he delivered a stinging rebuke, and he wondered if he was in for it again.

If so, he deserved it.

"My lady, I'm not sure what to do with this."

He presented her the book of music, and she juggled it with her mask and then looked up at him. "Country dances?"

"I, er, ran into Nancy in the music room. She'd come to fetch this, and then she left it behind. I imagine it's for the musicians."

The older woman blinked, glanced toward the drawing room he'd just come from, looked through to the music room, and then sent him a steely look.

"You were in the music room with Nancy? Alone?"

He nodded.

"How, I wonder, did that come about?"

"I, er, received a note from George, or perhaps Fitz, telling me she'd be there if I wanted to speak with her."

"The note was unsigned?"

"My lady." A maid came through from the back of the house, "Miss Cassandra needs—" She saw Simon and made a low curtsey.

"Thank you," she told the maid. "Tell her I'll be right along."

The maid hurried out, and Lady Loughton turned back to him.

"It's odd, don't you think?" she mused. "These are the usual dances played at every gathering. The musicians may know them by heart, and if they don't, they'll have their own music books." She glanced at the stairs leading up to the bedchambers. "I shall take care of these, your grace. Be sure to ring for help if you need a footman to assist you with dressing."

He bowed. "Thank you."

"Later on, you may wish to tell me what was said in the music room."

He felt the heat rising in his cheeks. "I do not know whether I shall live long enough or grovel low enough to make up for what I said and did at Lady Chilcombe's ball."

"Hmm." She nodded and a twinkle lit her eyes. "Nancy may be a gentle soul, but she's also a

Lovelace." She tapped him with her mask. "Be on your guard tonight, Simon."

She'd called him by his first name. That must be a good sign.

He watched her walk away, like the tiniest of elegant cutters, fast sailing, lightly armed, but quick-maneuvering and fierce.

CHAPTER SEVEN

The itching started as Simon descended the stairs for the party, and by the time he entered the garden, his back and shoulders begged to be scratched.

The perils of wearing garments pulled from an attic chest.

Still, a grown man did not scratch himself in public. One simply ignored the itch.

There were perhaps seventy-five guests assembled, or perhaps even more. The best thing about the masquerade was that he didn't have to go about being introduced to all and sundry. He bowed his head as he walked through the crowd, blissfully anonymous. Or, perhaps, given the low bows and deep curtsies, perhaps not. Perhaps the Swilling Duke scandal had blown over, and the respectable people of Leicestershire welcomed him.

He waved off a passing footman with a tray and, in the hopes that moving his body would ease the annoying prickling, made his way to a table where other servants were filling glasses from a giant punch bowl.

"Ah, your grace, is that you?" A man slapped his back, setting off a wave of tingles.

He recognized the voice and grin as George's.

"So much for the mask," Simon said. "I ought to dispense with the nuisance."

George laughed and handed him a brimming glass. "You're hard to miss. Quite the tallest guest here tonight."

"Aside from Percy."

"Ah, him." George waved a hand dismissively. "Where is your Hermia? Has she abandoned you already?"

He surreptitiously scratched his forearm. She wasn't *his* Hermia—er, Nancy. Not yet, but she would be. "I haven't seen Nancy yet. Only look there —that must be the fairy queen and her king."

George craned his neck and let out a wry chuckle. "That gown's indecent. Cass must have pulled it from the trunk with our great-grandmother's night clothes. It's a wonder Saulsfield allowed her to wear it."

Simon reached a hand back to his neck. If he could but just get a finger under his frilly collar...

"And there is Mother looking queenly with Fitz,

who is playing the ruler of Athens, and who will require Hermia's marriage or send her to a convent. Lovely crown, your majesty," he called and smiled slyly. "Wouldn't that be a tragedy, our Nancy confined to a convent."

George's baiting only served to enhance the physical irritation.

Simon steeled himself to resist the furious prickles along his shoulders and swiveled his head, the deuced mask restricting his peripheral vision. Lights twinkled and shimmered in the water of the bubbling center fountain.

Candles perched everywhere, in nooks and crannies, set against small mirrors and in punched-tin lanterns, while ropes strung with strips of thin tin stretched above, glittering in the light from the torches. The twangs and squeals of instruments being tuned came from the long terrace where the dancing would take place. In the parkland outside the garden, more torches surrounded a burning man, who'd be set afire later.

"Your sister did a bang-up job with the garden decorations," he said.

"There'll be drinking, dancing, eating. We'll have fireworks, and then the unmasking, and then those who are so inclined may have a midsummer bonfire," George said. "As long as we don't burn down the manor house, I'm content." He tugged at his coat collar. "I'm not keen on these costumes though. I'd rather have worn a toga, but Mel forbade wasting good bedsheets on costumes, and Mother concurred. Was there a coat to go with that peacock of a waistcoat you're wearing, your grace?"

"I dispensed with it. It was too tight." As was the waistcoat. He'd barely managed to button it. "And the shirt's damnably itchy." He shook a lacy cuff and then gave in to the need to scratch again. "You don't suppose your sister fished out a shirt for me that was infested?"

"Cass?" He shook his head. "No. But if it was Nancy—"

A figure in a tattered green shirt and a brown tunic flashed by tossing sparkles into the air, and behind him a winged fairy in white pulled streamers of shiny ribbons, while a small hobgoblin with horns tossed coal dust.

George shot a hand out for the hobgoblin and missed, and then cursed under his breath. "They've let the hellions out of the nursery," he said.

But Simon's attention was transfixed by the figure in green. Bounding onto a parapet, the creature waved and more sparkles flew, settling like pixie dust on the upturned faces below. Dark fairy wings caught the light and small horns adorned a knit cap pulled down like a knight's visor with eyeholes.

"James has arrived," George mused. "We're in for it from Puck. I'd best go and search out my wife, and then try to snatch up that hobgoblin and put him to bed."

"*I am that merry wanderer of the night, Robin Goodfellow.*" The green creature's voice carried across the garden, a melodic high tenor, silencing the crowd to murmurs. With an exaggerated bow, Puck sent another handful of sparkles, and then surveyed the crowd, pointing a wand at Saulsfield. "*I jest to Oberon and make him smile.*" He did a little jig on the narrow ledge, stumbled, and when the crowd gasped, laughed, and righted himself as if it had all been an act.

It was a long drop to the other side, Simon recalled.

"Is that one of the Lovelaces playing Puck and quoting Shakespeare?" A hand touched his own. Miss Hazelton leaned closer, her breast pressing into his itchy arm, and blast it, he didn't dare try to scratch it lest she accuse him of fondling her and try to force a marriage.

He took a step sideways, rubbed his arm, and looked her over. She wore the barest of masks; the barest of gowns as well, a white Grecian frock trimmed with a Greek key pattern. He'd wager there was naught but a thin chemise underneath.

"He's a daring fellow," she prompted, leaning in.

He would find himself sidestepping straight into the punch bowl if she kept this up.

"Why aren't you wearing side hoops?" he asked, unable to conceal the annoyance. The damn shirt was almost unbearable.

"Lady Saulsfield sent a gown up to me, but I had the foresight to bring my own costume." She cocked her head and smiled up at him. "I trust I will do as Helena. Do you like it?"

Any man liked getting an eyeful of a woman's body. As long as it wasn't his mother or sister, or—he thought of Nancy—his intended, publicly in the almost altogether.

"You don't like it." She made one of those oh-so-charming little moues that ladies must work to perfect.

A wave of itching coursed across his neck, and he spotted Percy making his way through the crowd. "Charming," he said. Especially charming if the sight distracted Percy from Nancy.

"*The fairy king doth keep his revels here tonight,*" Puck said. "*Take heed the queen come not within his sight.*"

"For shame, Puck," Cassandra, who was playing said fairy queen, called. "The Bard would lash you with his quill to see how you are using his words."

The guests laughed, and Puck pulled three acorns from a pocket and began to juggle them.

"Where is your Hermia?" Miss Hazelton asked.

Simon heard murmurs and turned toward the drinks table. A woman had stepped into the light, walking regally. She paused a moment and lowered her chin toward the servants, who stood, ladles and trays in hand, gawping and giggling, and then she continued her approach.

Hermia had arrived.

The gown... the gown was still dreadful with its tiny flowers on a yellowed white background and wide panniers. She'd added a lacy fichu to cover the lovely view she'd revealed in the music room, and her small bosom seemed even smaller. Perhaps she'd donned different stays to achieve that ramrod straight back and balance the wig, a massive white beehive dotted with pink bows.

With that dress, the wig perched on her head, and a mask concealing all but blue eyes and rouged lips, she stood in sharp contrast to Miss Hazelton.

Nancy must be as miserable in that uncomfortable get-up as he was in this shirt.

Miss Hazelton gasped and laughed, and the new arrival turned haughty blue eyes on her and struck a dramatic pose.

"*Helena, I understand not what you mean by this,*" the new lady said in a husky contralto, "*It seems that you scorn me.*"

"She's quoting Shakespeare too," someone nearby said.

Wonderful. They had an audience.

Miss Hazelton fell into the giggles. He would have laughed too if he didn't have to avoid offending Nancy, and if he didn't need to shed this damn shirt.

From his place on high, Puck put his fingers in his mouth and whistled, drawing the attention back to the figure on the garden wall. "Laughter?" he cried. *"Am I not he who frightens the maidens of the village? Hark."* He twirled his wand and pointed into the darkness. *"What hempen home-spuns have we swaggering here, so near the bower of the fairy queen?"*

Two figures in burlap tunics rushed into the light, their headpieces adorned with ass's ears and snouts. The guests erupted into laughter.

"Bottoms up." Puck pulled a glass from another pocket and mimed drinking.

A tall figure shouldered his way through to Simon.

"Sir Percy." Simon nodded to the new arrival.

Percy's eyes widened at the sight of Miss Hazelton. While his so-called friend was distracted by lust, Simon slid a hand under his own waistcoat and scratched.

You're welcome to the lady and her fortune.

Percy looked at Nancy, his lips quirking. "I say, blue eyes, right height… Miss Nancy, I presume? That's quite a, er, wig."

"A whole family of dormice might lodge there," Simon said.

No reaction. He'd hoped for a laugh or a scowl. Not that puzzled twist of her lips.

"Or other varmints," Simon said. "Does your shirt itch, Percy? This one is devilish uncomfortable."

The blue eyes under the beehive wig widened and then settled back into boredom.

It had only been a moment, but that reaction revealed something. Devil take it, the itching had him so addled he couldn't think what.

"*Bless thee, Bottoms, bless thee,*" Puck cried. "*Thou art translated.*"

The two asses heehawed and ran back out into the darkness.

"That's enough, Puck," Fitz called. "Gather your minions and take them back to the nursery."

Some of the guests shouted objections.

With an extravagant bow, Puck proclaimed, "*Lord, what fools these mortals be.*" Straightening, he directed his gaze at Simon.

Blue eyes, as blue as the eyes of the lady in panniers next to him. Not cold, bored, and amused, like hers, but blazing, almost fevered. The wand lifted, twirled enigmatically, and pointed straight at him, and a moment of battlefield panic flared. He'd stared down a French chasseur's barrel this closely.

And he'd picked himself up, fought on, and lived.

"*Jack shall have Jill, nought shall go ill.* But," the wand moved to Nancy. "*This is the woman,*" then back to Simon, "*but not this the man.*"

Simon's arm swung back and his glass shot through the air quick as a bullet.

Shock registered in Puck's blue eyes, and he ducked just in time, then stood tall, hand on his hips, and scoffed. *"I go, I go, look how I go. Swift as an arrow from the Tartar's bow."*

Then he bounded off to the other side and disappeared into the darkness.

Simon swiped at his neck again. That shot with the glass had been instinctive. He was glad James had dodged it, hoped the lad hadn't broken his neck on the long drop on the other side.

The guests clapped and cheered, and Fitz grinned and sent him a mock salute.

A waiter offered him another glass of punch, but he waved it away, and the servant moved on. No need to engender more attention with a Swilling Duke episode tonight.

"That was quite the Shakespeare performance," Percy said, smiling slyly. He leaned in close. "We know where Puck stands on the matchmaking," he whispered and then asked, "Shall I fetch you a drink, Miss Nancy?"

Dipping her eyes demurely a moment, she murmured a low thank you, and Percy strode off.

Something was amiss here.

A line of ants scurried along Simon's neck and down his back and arms. He wriggled his shoulders in the tight waistcoat trying to ease his skin, and saw Nancy's lips quirk.

And then he knew.

The dowager had warned him. The shirt wasn't infested with lice; he was the victim of a prank.

"That was gentlemanly of Sir Percy," Miss Hazelton said. "Except that he forgot me. I'm feeling parched myself." She rubbed against Simon again.

He turned on her. "Are you cold, Miss Hazelton? You must be cold in that thin gown. How the devil did the Greeks do it, running around in bedsheets. Excuse me, I'll tell one of the maids to fetch a shawl for you."

He stalked off into the house, unbuttoning the waistcoat as he went. This damned shirt had to come off.

UPSTAIRS IN HIS BEDCHAMBER, HE STRIPPED DOWN TO his waist, turned up the oil lamp and held the shirt close, shaking it. A powdery substance floated down to the floor.

Itching powder. He'd seen this trick before, more than once at school and again in the barracks. How...

Rose hips. She'd been carrying a basket of shriveled roses. Steamed and dried, the innards of the rose hips could be crushed into a devilish powder.

He covered his face and gave in to laughter. What a minx she was. He'd never have given her credit for something so devious. Though she'd probably had a good deal of help from her prancing, Shakespeare-quoting brother, James.

At the washstand, he lathered himself everywhere the shirt had touched, dripping all over the wooden flooring. There would be other schoolboy tricks tonight, for certain. Ridiculous, uncomfortable hijinks but probably not dangerous. As long as he was on alert, he'd be one step ahead.

He must temper his drinking and, well, his *temper*. He'd skated close to more scandal throwing the glass at James. What he'd really wanted to do was pull the lad down off the railing and give him a good schoolboy thumping.

This is the woman, but not this the man. There'd been fury in Puck's eyes, if not in his saucy tone.

Why? Why would James be angry over his sister's failed season? As much trouble as the lad had had at school, he'd be more likely to laugh at the Swilling Duke's jingle-brained blundering. He didn't seem the type to be passionate about his sister's honor, and he'd been nothing but cordial to Simon before dinner last night. In fact, when they'd chatted, James had seemed bored, amused even.

One set of eyes tonight had been bored and amused, the other blazing, almost fevered.

Hermia's small bosom was flatter than it had

been in the music room but that could be an illusion created by the fichu. The voices—they could be altered. Both in school and in the army, friends had donned gowns to play roles in theatricals. Without costumes, wigs, and masks, there was no way to mistake a man—or a boy James's age—for a grown woman.

But *with* costumes, wigs, and masks… Might they have switched?

He toweled himself dry, chuckling. One step ahead—that's where he'd stay.

* * *

NANCY GATHERED HER FAIRY, HER GOBLIN, AND HER two asses at the garden storage shed and had Arthur turn up the light on the lantern. Or was it Edward carrying the light? Both boys had shot up in the last year.

She shook off the thought and hugged Mary in one arm and Benjamin in the other.

"You did wonderfully tonight," she said.

"So did you." Edward laughed. "You could run away and go on the stage, Nancy."

Her breath froze. Had anyone seen her carry her valise to the folly?

"You fooled them, Nancy," Benjamin said, "but I don't think *we* did."

Mary nodded. "Papa knew it was me."

"All the grownups knew who you were, though I'm not sure they could tell Arthur and Edward apart." Nancy took a basket down from a shelf and smiled. Cook would have a fit tomorrow morning when there weren't enough eggs for breakfast, but this would be well worth it. "I don't think they truly minded you joining the fun, as long as you don't stay up all night, and as long as you don't do anything truly naughty."

"Like dropping eggs on his grace's head?" Edward asked, all innocence.

She'd seen Simon scratching his arms and chafing his neck. She'd also seen Miss Hazelton in an elegant toga *rubbing* against him.

Jealousy had struck then, and it flared again in her now.

She swallowed it down. Let the half-naked hussy have him.

"Whatever happens, the blame is on me," Nancy said. "What's the worst they can do to me?"

Especially if she was gone.

"They could send you to a convent," Edward said, "like the king threatened to do to Hermia in the play. We had to read *A Midsummer Night's Dream* last year."

"They could lock you up in your room," Arthur said.

Benjamin piped up. "And make you eat cold gruel for every meal."

Mary nudged her. "Or they could make you marry the Swilling Duke. I heard Papa talking to Mama about it."

Her stomach clenched and her mouth went dry, and she looked down into Mary's big blue eyes; eyes that were often *deceptively* innocent.

Never mind. The duke would have to catch her first.

Nancy touched the fair head. "Well, we shall make sure the *duke* doesn't want to marry *me*." She handed the basket to Benjamin. "We need to lure him to the old oak tree." It was their best climbing tree on the edge of the garden. "You and Mary need to get up top. Arthur and Edward will give you a boost to get started."

"And what are *our* orders after that, Puck?" Arthur asked, grinning.

"I know." Edward picked up his donkey head. "In the play, the fairy queen is besotted with Bottom. We'll go and bedevil Cass."

"Both of us?"

"Saulsfield is bound to grab one of us," Edward said. "It had better be you, Arthur. He won't birch an earl."

"No one will be birched." Nancy hoped. "Why not... why not chase the lady wearing the toga?"

"The see-through toga?" Arthur and Edward exchanged leering looks.

Heavens, they were only twelve and ogling women already. Were all males the same?

"Just don't distract the duke. We need James to—"

"Change of plans, sister." James hurried in, turning sideways through the narrow door. "The itching powder worked beautifully, and your performance was magnificent. I couldn't have done better. That is, until your last parting quip. The Swilling Duke is on to us, Nancy. We must switch costumes."

CHAPTER EIGHT

Switch costumes? After all the trouble she'd gone to?

"No."

"Yes. Don't you see? He's not at all foxed—barely touched that drink he threw at you—but he's in a devil of a miff over the itching powder. Any minute, he'll pull Mama or Fitz over and accuse you of being me in disguise. But if we switch now—what a scene you can make of it when he discovers you're you. He'll look like a widgeon to all and sundry, and you'll have him on his knees, like the worst sort of jingle-brain. And it'll spare you Mama's wrath, as well."

Nancy thought about Simon with Miss Hazelton hanging on him, and that fortune-hunting gudgeon, Sir Percy. She'd already given her main performance. As Puck, she couldn't do more than run in and run out for the rest of the evening before one of her brothers grabbed her.

As Hermia, she could stand regally and snipe at the Swilling Duke and his court, and the panniers would provide an adequate barrier against Sir Percy's groping.

"All right," she said. "We'll do it."

* * *

THE SOUND OF A COUNTRY DANCE REACHED SIMON'S ears as he descended the staircase and made his way back to the party, a scheme in mind.

On the terrace, the dance had just ended. Cassandra spotted him and hurried over.

"Your costume," she exclaimed. "What happened?"

"I found it didn't suit," he said, "but look, I'm wearing my mask."

"I expected better from you, Swillingstone, and dash it all, I fear it may rain. Mama is inside arranging to move the musicians indoors after this set." She glanced over his shoulder. "But look, there is Miss Hazelton, who turned her nose up at the costume I prepared for her coming our way."

He took Cassandra's hand and placed it over his arm.

"Then by all means, you must dance with me, Lady Saulsfield."

Miss Hazelton frowned and joined the dance with one of the local men, and as she and her partner worked their way down the line of dancers, she threw Simon a saucy look and demanded the next dance.

"Tell her Nancy is your next partner," Cassandra said. "Only where is she? I haven't seen her dancing yet. Though James has flown through several times."

"Puck?" he asked innocently, wondering whether she knew of her siblings' deception.

"Yes. His performance was just brilliant, wasn't it? So diverting, and nothing that I planned. Do not tell him that I complimented him though. He'll be impossible for the rest of his stay."

"Perhaps I should ask Puck to dance with me," he said.

She laughed and tapped him with her fan, and then they separated for a turn with the couple across from them.

When the dance ended, Cassandra announced the plan to move the dancing indoors and the musicians began packing up. Looking around, Simon saw Miss Hazelton eyeing him. Footmen refilled glasses and the general tenor of the party grew more boisterous.

George and Fitz stood near the balustrade looking out into the darkness beyond the twinkling lights.

"What's afoot?" Simon asked the brothers. "Guests misbehaving?"

George raised an eyebrow. "You changed your coats? And your shirt as well, I see."

Simon accepted a drink from a passing footman. "Itching powder."

George and Fitz exchanged grins, and both men laughed out loud.

"Did I miss a joke?" Sir Percy sidled up.

Just then, a figure in green bumped through them. Puck elbowed Sir Percy, jostled against Simon, righted his drink for him with a saucy grin, and then ducked away from the Lovelace men, snickering.

"Can't catch me," Puck cried.

The two boys wearing donkey heads dived between Puck and the footman juggling a tray. Laughing, they veered off, one running to Cassandra, the other halting Miss Hazelton. They tossed handfuls of white powder and flower petals upon each of their quarries. Miss Hazelton's tormentor dodged around tossing more powder, eluding the hands reaching for him, and laughing.

She fell against Simon, jostling his drink again. "Well, I never," she said, and sneezed powerfully.

"I haven't touched this." Simon handed his drink to Percy, set her away from him, and pulled out his handkerchief. She took it and held it up to her nose, sneezed again, and then, eyes rounded, face turning red, choked, trying to hold back another series of sneezes.

"Catch him." Simon flung out a hand toward the laughing Bottom, but the boy sped away into the darkness.

Miss Hazelhurst tossed the handkerchief to the flagstones, stomped on it, and waggled her hand. "A drink..."

Percy had taken a healthy swallow of the punch, but he gave the rest to Miss Hazelton, who quaffed it in one gulp and then choked some more.

George picked up Simon's handkerchief, held it up to his nose and pinched his nostrils together holding back a sneeze. "White pepper," he said, grinning.

"I've caught one of them." Saulsfield had a grip on the Bottom, who'd left Cassandra in a sneezing fit.

"Your boy, Edward, Fitz, or my Lord Glanford?" George asked.

Fitz rubbed his chin, trying not to smile. "Devilish hard to say whether it's your Arthur or our little brother, Edward. Let's allow Saulsfield to do the unveiling. He can decide the punishment."

"No," Cass said, patting her nose. "Don't punish him. There's no harm done. Why, Miss Hazelton, it's only a little sneezing."

The heiress had found another handkerchief somewhere and had it pressed to her face.

Saulsfield pulled the tie on the ass's head and

lifted it off. "Lord Glanford," he laughed. "How can I whip an earl, Loughton? He outranks me."

Cassandra kissed Arthur's cheek prettily and thanked him for adding excitement to the party.

"Earl or no, you must answer for this, Arthur," George said, his voice genial.

There was no better person to raise a titled young man, Simon thought, and perhaps no better friend—if he could keep him—to help a new duke.

George eyed his stepson. "Where, pray tell, are your coconspirators?"

"Yes, where is Nancy?" Sir Percy's eyes glowed under his mask, his stare more predatory than usual.

"I did *say* I wouldn't tell, sir." Arthur straightened. "But I didn't *promise*. We were meeting under the big oak tree. The one at the edge of the garden."

Sir Percy blinked and sped off.

"Dash it all," Simon said, tearing off his mask.

Two pairs of hands held him back. "That was too easy," Fitz said.

"I feel faint," Miss Hazleton whined.

Simon shook them both off and ran. He knew that look in his friend Percy's eyes. He'd pulled the battle-crazed dastard off a woman after a fierce siege in Spain. Percy would see soon enough that Hermia was a boy, and then what?

There'd been no battle here tonight, but... the drink. Puck—Nancy—had bumped into him and jostled his drink.

What in Hades had she dosed it with?

* * *

NANCY STOOD IN A CIRCLE OF LANTERNS AND glanced up at the spot of white in the tree that was Mary.

"I hear them," Benjamin said in a loud whisper, and Mary giggled.

Adjusting her fichu, Nancy straightened her back, wondering if James had put itching powder in the gown. Underneath, she wore only the hoops and Puck's trousers, James having worn his own slimmer trousers under the dress. Now, without a chemise, which James had disdained wearing, the stiff brocade of the bodice and hastily pinned stomacher rubbed the sensitive skin of her shoulders and breasts.

In the few minutes spared her for dressing, she'd had a devil of a time shoving her long hair under the heavy wig. The blighted thing listed and swayed with each step like an ocean wave. How appropriate that her great-grandmother's generation had topped their wigs with boats.

The music had stopped, and a drizzle had started. A pity that they couldn't control the weather. The rain would diminish their audience and dampen the Swilling Duke's embarrassment over their next prank.

"They're coming," James said, breaking through the bushes. "Strike your pose, Hermia."

"Oof." One of the asses collided with James. "Miss Hazelton is in high dudgeon with the sneezing, but the duke gave the drink to Sir Percy, and they've got Arthur."

"It won't be long," James said. "Your pose, Hermia."

A flicker of unease stirred in her. Nancy set her hands to the tops of the sidehoops. "What drink?"

Footsteps crunched down the gravel path. "Tell you later." James grabbed Edward and they scurried behind the tree.

"You'd better," she muttered, turning her attention to her role. First, she'd lure the duke into his egging and enjoy the spectacle, then the boys would distract him while she vanished into the night.

It was a pity she'd miss watching him return to the party with egg on his face, hair, coats, and anywhere else the minions could target.

"Here he comes," Mary called from the tree.

Would Simon arrive alone, or would her brothers come with him? Or might they simply send footmen to haul Nancy away?

A gust of damp wind swirled around her neck and set her teeth chattering. Or was it her nerves causing the rattling?

She forced in a deep breath and held herself still

while a bad feeling came over her and her feet itched to take immediate flight.

The approaching footsteps grew louder, and a man burst through the break in the hedge.

Fustian. It was that jackanapes, Sir Percy.

"Mish Nanshy." Sir Percy halted a few feet in front of her, not quite in perfect range under the tree. He bowed, never taking his eyes off her, then he cast off his coat.

Goosebumps ran up and down her back. She should back away, make him advance; he deserved a good egging too. But apprehension froze her in place.

He straightened and slithered closer, unbuttoning his long waistcoat, yanking it off, and then proudly cocking a pose and pointing to—

She gasped, confusion turning to indignation, and then to white hot anger that drove out any fear. *How dare he.* He couldn't be that drunk or that dishonorable that he'd...

The aphrodisiac. She'd stowed the packet in one of Puck's tunic pockets to keep it out of James's hands and had forgotten to remove it when they'd switched costumes.

Her hands curled into fists at her hips.

"What have you done, James?"

She still wore her half boots. One kick to Sir Percy's bollocks, and another to her brother's arse, and then she'd be off.

"Shir Pershy, ma dear, at your shervishe." The fool leaned closer and leered. "Don't be shy, Mish Nanshy."

Simon rushed into the clearing. "Hold there, Percy." He made a grab for the sot, missing him.

Nancy took one step back.

"Go away, Clayding. Mish Nanshy ish mine." Sir Percy reached for her, and she dodged back again, outside the circle of lanterns, watching him fight for his balance.

"Are you sure this is Miss Nancy?" Simon asked, coyly.

James had been right; Simon had uncovered their ruse.

Fury seized her. Both reprobates were in perfect range now.

Leaves rustled and Miss Hazelton stumbled in, knocking over a lantern and throwing herself at Simon.

"Your grashe," she cried and grabbed for him.

Simon's captured arm flailed, but Miss Hazelton clung to it like a hound clutching a fat bird.

The hussy. Nancy glanced up at the spot of white. She'd give the signal herself if—

Sir Percy lunged drunkenly. Nancy jumped back, tripped, and plopped onto her bottom, caught awkwardly between her two side hoops.

"*Now.*" The shout came from behind the tree.

As Sir Percy staggered again for balance, an egg

dropped onto his head. Another hit his shoulder. He swore, brushing at the sticky messes.

More eggs dropped. Sir Percy dodged and swore more, Simon brushed at the shells and grabbed for Sir Percy, and Miss Hazelton screamed curses Nancy had never heard before, not even from one of her brothers.

Laughing, James and Edward appeared on either side of Nancy and hauled her up.

"What did you give them," she hissed.

"Shhh," James said. "It was only a bit of Spanish fly."

She grabbed James's shoulders and shook him. "I told you—"

"She'sh mine," Sir Percy said drunkenly.

"The duke didn't have any," Edward whispered. "I swear I saw him hand away the glass without taking a sip."

"Dear duke." Miss Hazelton still clenched Simon's arm. "Make me yoursh."

With her free hand, the hussy ripped the shoulder of her toga. The gown floated down to her waist. James and Edward both gasped and then erupted into giggles.

"I'm going to thrash the both of you when this is over," Nancy said.

James choked and caught his breath. "Maybe we should run away with you tonight, Nancy."

Her breath caught.

"We know," Edward whispered.

"Get off, both of you," Simon bellowed. "You're like dogs in heat." He was still struggling to shake free of Miss Hazelton and tugging Sir Percy back by his neckcloth.

One more egg plopped, a direct hit on one of Miss Hazelton's bared breasts. She screeched, tore away from Simon, and turned on Nancy. "You... you... you harpy."

Nancy's throat clogged with a mixture of laughter and incipient tears. Miss Hazelton, naked, egg-soaked and lust-filled—if she had the skill to draw a caricature, this one would sell well in the London shops.

Yet she pitied the young woman, throwing herself at Simon, baring herself in front of the men and boys. When the poison wore off, would Miss Hazelton have the sense or the character to be embarrassed?

Or... would Simon have to marry her to save her reputation?

Trembling, Nancy grabbed James and shook him. "Whatever you do, make this right or you'll shame Mama and Mel."

"You'll shame them more with what you're planning."

She shook her head, blinking back tears. "I left notes."

* * *

HIS ARM FINALLY FREE, SIMON BRUSHED AN EGGSHELL from his shoulder. Miss Hazelton was as frenzied as Percy. Of course—she'd downed the rest of that poisoned cup.

Simon looked at Puck, he looked at Hermia. He returned to the laughing, carefree blue eyes of Puck, then caught the startled, nay, angry eyes of Hermia. Surely those were tears in her eyes shining in the lanternlight.

He'd got it wrong. It was James who'd dropped something into the drink he'd handed to Percy. Nancy would never doctor his drink; she'd already made it clear she didn't want him to pursue her.

While he gripped Percy, Miss Hazelton surged past them, dodged Puck and Bottom, and yanked the wig from Nancy's head. Hair, rich, thick, and golden, tumbled down to her waist.

"What the devil?" Fitz had appeared. An egg splashed on his coat sleeve and giggling erupted above. "Mary," he bellowed, "get out of that tree. You too, Benjamin."

Percy tore out of Simon's grip and turned on him. Simon ducked just in time, dodging a blow.

"Run, Nancy," Puck said in a stage whisper.

Nancy disappeared into the night and Percy charged after her, and then sprawled face down in the dirt. Puck grinned, pulled his foot back, and while the villain tried to rise, Bottom tripped Miss Hazelton. She staggered, reached out a hand, and collapsed onto Percy, knocking him to the ground again.

Percy's gaze traveled over her. His eyes flared, and his arms locked around her.

Simon snatched Puck by the arm and pulled off his mask. "You," he said, "you jackanapes. You tampered with my drink. I ought to thrash you. Do you have an emetic in your bag of tricks?"

James grinned and nodded.

"Then you'd best give Percy and Miss Hazelton some, or you'll find yourself with a noose around your neck for poisoning them."

"It's not—"

"What did you give them?"

"It's only the tiniest bit of Spanish—"

He shook James. "The emetic. Now."

"Yes, duke."

"When this is settled, I'll buy your commission. You can employ your tricks fighting the King's enemies."

"I'm too young."

"I don't care if you have to go as a drummer boy, you're ready."

The two little ones had come down from the tree and stood, mouths gaping, at the couple rolling together on the ground. "Turn around, both of you. You too, Edward," Fitz growled.

Simon shook James. "Where is Nancy running to?" he asked.

"The folly," James said, laughter in his gaze. "If you hurry, she may still be there," he added in a whisper.

And where would she run to next? He dropped the lad's arm.

"Wait, Simon," Fitz said. Footsteps crunched as three footmen joined them, and Fitz gave orders. "Pull those two off each other, one of you give her your coat, and get them back to the house without either of the Ladies Loughton seeing them. James, go with them and dose them with the emetic. Simon, if you'll take these two back to the nursery before you clean up, I'll go and retrieve Nancy. Or perhaps I should just let her stew at the folly all night and bring her back in the morning."

"She won't be there in the morning," Mary said. "She packed a bag and took it there earlier. She's running away."

"She's going to France," Benjamin said.

"*France?*" Simon cried.

"Mrs. Simpkins' tour." Fitz shook his head. "Mother ought to have…" He crouched down in front of his daughter. "You've been spying, Mary. What else do you know?"

"She's going to Birmingham first, so she can join the troupe. Wasn't she good? She fooled you all." Mary glanced over her shoulder. "Except you, duke, so James made her swap places again. Can we turn around now?"

His instincts had been right after all. He'd seen Nancy through the mask.

The thought cheered him. He *knew* Nancy. Would get to know her better as the years went by, and perhaps, there'd be very few dull moments.

He swiped a drip of egg yolk from his forehead. "I'll go and find her."

"Clean yourself up first," Fitz said. "I'll send someone to watch the gate and put somebody at the Swan as well. There won't be a coach until morning."

Mary shook her head. "You won't know her. She'll be in disguise. She took some of Uncle James's clothing."

Nancy could change, scale the boundary wall, and walk until she got a lift on a farm cart to another coaching inn. She'd be frightened but she'd do it anyway, the brave girl.

"I'll go now." Simon stalked off. Nancy might go downstream to the bridge to cross, or upstream to the rock crossing where the children had been playing in the morning. Either way, it would take her a while.

He needed to wash anyway. At the edge of the lake, he cast off his coats and shoes and dove in.

CHAPTER NINE

*T*he sole of her half boot slipped on the first rock, and she cursed, wishing for a lantern. Clouds covered the night sky and hid what little light she'd get from the quarter moon. The drizzle had turned to gentle rain that nevertheless seeped into her bodice and skirt.

Still, she'd crossed this way so many times she should know the stones by heart and—

Her foot slid and twisted and she slipped into the water up to her hip. She clung to the rock, her nails raking the cold stone for purchase. The sodden brocade dragged yet she managed to crawl up and seat herself.

She ought to have shed the skirt and hoops before crossing. Now, the soaked ties would have to be cut, and her knife was packed away in her bag at the folly.

Tears threatened again as she thought of Simon. Simon with Miss Hazelton. And the execrable Percy Nacton? Someone would come after her, but she felt certain Fitz wouldn't allow Percy to do so. Nor Simon, or anyone else who might compromise her. And she wasn't at all certain her brothers would rouse themselves to come tonight, unless Mama insisted.

And she might. Her mother's refusal to allow her to meet Sally in London had surprised her. The argument over visiting Sally in Birmingham... that had broken her heart. Mama could be strict but she'd never been unreasonable and unfair and so high in the instep. If Sally was respectable enough for Mrs. Thomas's academy, why couldn't she visit her?

No, her mother wouldn't make escape easy, and if she learned of the aphrodisiac, Nancy would never be allowed any sort of freedom, ever again. Never mind that it was her beef-witted brother's fault.

It had all slipped out of her control, and the rest would as well if she spent too much time thinking. She'd best make haste, change quickly, and go as far as her feet would carry her.

A NOT SO SHORT WHILE LATER, DRENCHED AND miserable, she dragged herself and her wet skirts up the steps of the pillared portico and found the door to the folly locked. She rattled the knob, certain she'd left it unlocked, and with a sharp oath, sunk to the flagstones and gave into the tears of frustration and rage she'd been fighting. Simon—what had she done, driving him into the arms of Miss Hazelton? And… James had almost poisoned him, and it was her own fault for asking his help.

* * *

INSIDE THE FOLLY, SIMON HEARD THE DOOR RATTLE and he chuckled.

He'd locked it, a retaliatory prank of his own. If she broke a window to enter, he'd cover the cost of replacement. It would be worth it to see how determined she'd be.

She would find a way to enter, he was certain.

Inside the folly, he'd had time to light candles, close curtains, and kindle a fire, before chucking off his wet shirt and stockings and rubbing himself down with a dry blanket he'd found in the side bedroom. The folly was far more elegant than it had been during his visits so many years earlier.

A valise, stuffed with a gown and the delicate white cloth of a lady's underthings, had been stowed in a cabinet. A huge hamper of food and wine sat on a table in the main room. The valise must be the one Mary said Nancy had brought over earlier. But the hamper—how she'd managed to bring that, and how she'd carry it with her, if that was her plan, he had no idea.

He went to the door, pressed his ear to the panel, and waited.

The sound of sobbing, followed by choking, then angry cursing, sent his emotions tumbling with memories of his mother, a woman who, when all other means of persuasion proved fruitless, fell back on piteous weeping to get her way.

He shook off the thought. This was Nancy and she couldn't know he was here.

With a soft click he turned the key in the well-oiled lock and opened the door.

Her head shot up, her mouth fell open, and she stumbled to her feet, looking not at all happy to see him. "S-simon?" She choked in a breath. "H-how... *You're* here?"

Light from the open door revealed tear-ravaged eyes under tendrils of wet hair. Her clothes were soaked as well, more so than from just the rain. He longed to take her into his arms, like...

The full memory flooded him, the sensations, the overwhelming desire he'd almost succumbed to when he'd kissed her at Lady Chilcombe's.

The wild hair, the clinging skirts, the sheer vulnerability—she was just as desirable now, even more so.

"Did you swim across?" he asked, forcing a placid tone.

She shuddered and shook her head. "I s-slipped and f-fell in. If you must know."

"You crossed on the rocks?"

With an irritated frown, she nodded, and he quashed a wave of tenderness. Her pride was smarting. "Anyone would slip on a night like this. You'll want to get out of those wet things."

She blinked, her gaze lingering on his bare chest, traveling over his trousers to his bare feet and up again. Even in the dim light he saw her color rising, stirring his own desire.

Damping down his urges, he smiled. "As it happened, since I was bound to be soaked by the rain anyway, I took the quickest way and swam across. Excuse my deshabille. I've started a fire for us." He stood aside and gestured for her to enter, and then saw her hesitation.

"You're safe with me, Nancy. The Swilling Duke is not present, just me, Simon."

She'd lost her fichu and the stomacher, wet and weighed down by ornate beading, sagged. He could see the top of her nipples, pebbled, pert, and beckoning. Her hair streamed down to her waist in passionate disarray.

As she stood biting her lower lip, desire made a liar out of him. How safe was she when lust was flooding him, hot and urgent?

He gripped the edge of the door to keep from reaching for her. "Can we begin again, my love? Like old times? Your brother's friend, a soldier, an unworthy clerk's son courting his best friend's sister, a baron's daughter?"

A shiver went through her and echoed in his heart, deeper than his lust, purer than his desire. This lovely girl was meant to be his, he knew it for certain. He just had to convince her as well.

"We're not courting, S-simon." She swept past, defiant in her sodden skirt, splashing his bare feet as she shoved the awkward hoops through the door.

* * *

NANCY SCANNED THE ROOM AS SHE WALKED TO THE beckoning warmth of the hearth. Candles brightened the soft angles of this central parlor, shimmered in mirrors, and cast shadows over carved wainscotting and Turkey carpets. In her hurried visit that morning, she'd barely noticed the remodeled décor. That basket, with bread and tall bottles protruding, had most certainly not been here. If Simon swam across, it must have been delivered earlier.

She squeezed back another rush of angry tears. Someone else would appear here tonight. Some couple seeking the romance of the folly—Fitz and Mel, probably. The restoration had been Fitz's project after all, his gift to Mel.

She leaned her forehead against the warming

mantel. Tangle on top of tangle—when Fitz arrived, she would be safe from this half-naked Simon, with his gorgeous bare chest and beautiful bare feet, and the tight trousers that hugged his legs and showed... everything. How could a girl not notice?

She'd be trapped. Fitz wouldn't let her sneak off into the night, and until he arrived, she'd still have to deal with Simon. Getting him drunk would take too long. Bashing him on the head—she couldn't do it. She hated that James had almost poisoned him. Humiliating Simon, thrashing him even, yes, but she couldn't do him real harm.

Still, she must somehow get rid of him, if she wanted to leave.

If she wanted to leave.

Can we begin again, my love? What did he mean, his *love*?

Oh, how she wanted that to be more than just some courtly lie to get at her dowry, that he could want her as much as she wanted him.

Or, as much as she'd once wanted him. She'd known him most of her life, yet they were barely acquainted, as his behavior at Lady Chilcombe's ball had proven.

Men were another species of humans.

"Do you need help with those skirts?" The melting baritone tickled her ear and sent another shiver through her.

Her wet, stringy hair lifted. A warm blanket came

around her shoulders and she hugged it to her, wanting to weep for the tenderness, knowing she must resist if she truly wanted to leave.

Turning, she raised her eyes. Dark hair plastered his forehead and neck. The egg yolk had washed away in the lake, but even from this distance, he smelled like pondwater.

Or maybe it was her own self she smelled. The thought made her smile, and her smile triggered an answering one from him that set butterflies aflutter inside her.

Light from the candles danced and flickered over wide shoulders, sculpted muscles, and a sprinkling of dark hair between the manly flat nipples of Simon's chest. Her heart raced as she fought the force pulling her toward him.

"Does this dress tie?" he asked, matter-of-factly, studying her gown and breaking the spell. "Or are there hooks?"

"The skirts and hoops tie. They're so wet, I may have to cut them."

He gave her a long look. "Is there a knife in your bag? That is your bag in the cupboard, isn't it?"

So, he'd found her valise. There'd be no sneaking away.

"Yes," she hissed.

He tucked the blanket more securely. "Wait here. I'll find it."

In the end, he carried the valise over to a table for

her, and with the scissors from her small sewing kit, she freed herself and pushed down the skirt, petticoat and panniers to find Simon watching.

He'd given her no privacy, but it didn't matter. There'd been no privacy in the shed where they'd changed, and anyway, the dress bodice covered her to her waist, and she still wore Puck's trousers.

Her boot stuck in a hoop, and she wobbled. Strong hands caught her and lifted her, freeing her from the frivolous boning.

"Trousers." He laughed, setting her back. "Puck's trousers?"

His eyes darkened, as they had just before he'd kissed her that night so many weeks ago. His hands slid down to her waist and sent heat sizzling through her. A log crackled, like the magnetic force hissing between them.

She nodded.

"Sit down. Let's get you out of those wet boots."

His tone brimmed with kindness, not seduction. She sat and watched him patiently work the wet laces and ease off the half boots. When his fingers reached under the trousers and hooked the top of her stockings, the shock of his touch sizzled through her and she held her breath.

Their gazes met and her heart hammered in her chest. He tossed the stockings aside, stood, and took her hands. "You'll want to change."

"Yes." She set her hands to his—those strong hot

hands, with their long fingers—pried them away, and went to rummage through her bag.

Should she don the rest of the boy's clothes she'd brought for her travel, or a gown, or... her nightgown?

Not the nightgown. That would tempt them both, and she needed to send Simon away. She needed him to not follow her. Sally was expecting her; had promised she'd get her mother to take her in.

They'd decided it would be safer for Nancy to travel alone as a boy and there'd be no time to waste changing clothes again after Simon left.

She found the clothing she needed, snatched up a candle, and hurried off to one of the side rooms.

Inside, she gasped. She hadn't had time to explore the folly rooms in the morning. Here, in what used to be a storage room filled with castoff furniture and other things, a wide tester bed took center stage. Pale ivory hangings reflected the candlelight and framed the rich red and ivory of the bedding and Aubusson carpet.

Family legend said the folly was built as a private love nest by her great-great grandfather for his new bride. Fitz and Mel were restoring the tradition. Theirs was a love match; how she envied them.

When she returned to the main room, she found Simon setting out plates and silverware. An open bottle of wine stood next to two wineglasses.

He looked up from the table, blinked, and his eyes crinkled in a mischievous smile. "You make a fetching boy, though the hair is a distraction."

"I'll pin it up when it's dry." She needed to unsnarl it as well.

"I'll play your maid and brush it for you, but come and eat first. You packed a good cold collation."

He uncovered a plate of cold meats, and despite the butterflies flapping in her stomach, her mouth watered. She'd need sustenance to carry her through the night. Boarding the coach at the Royal Swan was not a possibility now that her family knew of her plans. If she couldn't get a lift on a farm cart, it would be a long walk to the next coaching inn.

Suddenly exhausted, she plopped into the chair he'd pulled out. "I didn't pack that basket, which means someone else is coming—perhaps Fitz and Mel. Go back before they arrive, Simon. You don't want to be found here with me."

"Don't I?" His lips quirked. They were firm lips, but the almost grin, the piercing heat in his eyes, made her even more nervous.

Her hands fisted. "You drank the Spanish fly too."

"No. Not a drop. Percy grabbed my drink and he shared it with Miss Hazleton when the sneezing powder seized her."

A shudder went through her. "I told my brother, no aphrodisiacs."

"If James thought to give *me* an aphrodisiac—which, by the way, I'd never need with you—do you think perhaps he was working against you? Perhaps with whoever delivered this basket of food?"

"No…"

Her stomach lurched and she buried her face in her hands. *Arrgh, her interfering family.*

The damp smell of the yellowed paper she'd found in the attic came back to her. *Be careful what you wish for.*

She'd wished to have her revenge and then slip away into the night and begin her adventure. She'd had *some* revenge. She'd slipped away into the night. And this… being alone with Simon in a love nest was certainly an adventure but not the one she'd planned. Or wanted?

They could make you marry the Swilling Duke. I heard Papa talking to Mama about it.

She rubbed her forehead and studied her empty plate. "I'll not be forced into marriage."

Wine gurgled and splashed into a glass. "Much as I want you, Nancy, I would never force you."

She glanced up at him, then tried to look away and couldn't. A thin scar marked his side and another one his upper arm, while dark hair sprinkled his chest and ran down to the top of his trousers.

"S-simon, you can't stay here. You need to go."

"And as soon as I leave, you'll run away? You were planning to run away, weren't you?"

"I'm not running away. I'm simply leaving, which I won't be able to do if I'm locked in my bedchamber. I need to go before Fitz arrives here."

"Fitz sent me after you."

"*Fitz?*"

"Yes. No one else is coming tonight. Eat." He took her plate and filled it with meat, salads, and bread. "And then I'll escort you to Birmingham myself."

"How did you—"

"Mary told us, the imp. As it happens, the Duke of Swillingstone has a small hunting box near Marston Green. In fact, I've just come from there. I saw the notice about Mrs. Simpkins' concert. She's going on to France and Italy, I hear. Were you planning to accompany her there?"

* * *

Simon watched as shock registered on her face and color flowed up from under the poorly tied neckcloth to flood her cheeks.

It was hard to keep a straight face. "Don't be angry with diabolical little Mary."

She spluttered and threw down her fork. "Is it so terrible that I want to visit a school friend? That, perhaps, I might see something besides Loughton Hall and London ballrooms? Yes. I would dearly love to travel to France with Sally and her mother. I love plays, the theater, learning lines and playing a r-role. I want to travel."

Traveling to France and playing a role. He stowed those bits away. "Catch your breath. Have a sip of wine and then go on. Tell me more about what you want."

Head hanging, she sighed, blinked rapidly under her angry flush, and tossed back the wine.

What she wanted wasn't so unreasonable. Yet he understood completely her family's worries. There were too many men like Percy Nacton about.

There might be other men like himself, drunkenly groping her at a ball. She was young, beautiful, and rich; all those blessings restricted her freedom. Just as this new title restricted his. He couldn't dump everything and run off to the far parts to fight the Crown's enemies. People here were relying on him.

He refilled her glass. "How little freedom any of us truly has."

She scoffed. "You have plenty of freedom to come and go. *You* can associate with actresses. Why, an actress was Fitz's first mistress."

"Nancy." He couldn't help a shocked laugh. He and George and their friends at school had been all abuzz with that gossip. "You would have been a baby when... if that happened."

"It did happen, and I know because Sally told me.

The woman was a friend of her mother. A Frenchman became her next protector. They fell in love. She went on to marry him and move to Paris."

And they lived happily ever after. Oh God, surely Nancy wasn't romanticizing the life of a courtesan? For every ladybird that was happily married there were a hundred that wound up poor and poxed.

How to tell her that without starting an argument?

"Fitz went on to marry horrid Alice and be mostly miserable, though he adores his daughter by her. The little eavesdropping tattletale."

"You adore her too."

"She's far too clever. But yes, I love her."

"Love," he said, thinking, "can be a rare thing, in marriage, in families. You have a loving family, Nancy."

"A loving family who never listen to me, except at keyholes. Fitz and George are probably standing on the opposite shore passing a spyglass back and forth. Unless they're outside right now. I must go."

When she started to rise, he pulled his chair close to hers and nudged her back into her seat. "When did you last eat?" He cut through a slice of beef. "You need your strength. I won't stop you from leaving."

She opened her mouth and accepted the meat, eyeing him sidewise and chewing.

"I won't let you travel alone though." What had Fitz said about the actress, Nancy's friend's mother?

"I'm not sure Mrs. Simpkins would happily receive a runaway dressed as a boy. It's said that she's taken great pains over her respectability for the sake of her daughter."

Nancy turned quickly away and chased the food down with a swallow of wine.

"While you eat, I'll tell you a story about the night the Swilling Duke made his first appearance to the *ton*."

CHAPTER TEN

*H*er blue eyes flashed an icy anger that made him want to squirm. "Even drunk, my brothers would never behave the way you did. What were you thinking?"

How to convince her? He might as well start with the truth. "At that moment when I spotted you, I was thinking that you were someone else I'd met earlier that evening. Someone who'd followed me to the ball. Someone less respectable. I wondered if, perhaps, town balls were somewhat, er, shabby affairs." He forked a pickled vegetable onto her plate. "I need help, Nancy. My time at school, my visits here, even the etiquette of the officers' mess—none of those showed me how to navigate nobility. Can we begin again, Nancy? Can you show me how to find my way in your world?"

"*My* world?"

"Yes. You're from a titled family. My parents were generations removed from the dukedom. My father was a humble clerk, and my mother a farmer's daughter. They scraped together the money for my schooling so I could at least claim to be a gentleman. After they died, I had barely enough income to buy my kit and pay mess fees. A baron's daughter was out of my reach."

"And a duke is out of mine."

"No. And before you bring it up, I know all about the dowry, and that it will be yours to do as you please with."

"Only if I marry." She shook her head. "I'm leaving. If you must know, I'm going to get up the nerve to ask Mrs. Simpkins to help me gain an audition. I can memorize lines and project my voice. I can act. I can't do any of that if I'm making the social rounds of the *ton*."

"*This is the woman, but not this the man.*" He watched as her color rose again.

"Yes, and then you threw a glass at me."

"In my defense, I didn't know it was you then. And you were wrong on both counts. You pointed to James, and he was certainly not the woman. And I—"

"You are *not* the man for me, your grace."

Her glare dared him to contradict her. He held her gaze while her breathing accelerated to short puffs and his own heartbeat picked up. She was going to be a challenge, a delicious, spirited challenge. A girl he knew so little and yet so well.

He touched her hot cheek, and a small gasp parted her lips.

"Let me prove to you that I am. Let me court you. Give me four weeks."

Frowning, she swallowed hard and shook her head. "No. I'm not the woman for you. Dukes make practical matches. You have your freedom to go where you want and do what you want. You can spend your nights in a gaming hell. You can, and probably will, take lovers. I don't want a husband like that."

"And I don't want to be a husband like that. I want to cherish my wife and have children, and a happy home. I want you, Nancy, now and forever."

Her eyes grew shiny and her mouth trembled. "You say that now. But only love could make a duke be faithful to his duchess, and you can't p-possibly be in love with me."

"I can and will be faithful with you by my side. Give me a chance, Nancy. Here is my proposal: we'll begin our formal courtship in Birmingham, properly chaperoned. And we'll end the four weeks with a wedding, and then travel to my villa in Provence."

A light flared in her eyes, and he knew he'd hooked her. He only needed to hold back the swelling of his head over those words, *my villa*, and the swelling of his, er, more private parts, which threatened to triumph over his willpower tonight.

He took a breath, damped down his desire, and went on. "Yes. I have a villa in Provence. We'll spend our honeymoon there. And in between, you'll learn the lines for the role of a lifetime, the Duchess of Swillingstone."

She bit her lip then frowned, apparently speechless. Her mouth opened, as if the two plump lips were begging him to lean in and savor them. They would get to that, and very soon.

Before she could muster words, he jumped in.

"The less formal courtship we'll begin tonight while we have these hours together. You'll go to the altar a virgin, my love, but not an ignorant one."

* * *

HIS WARM LIPS TOUCHED HERS IN A KISS SO TENDER, she shivered against him, and without thinking, opened her mouth to welcome him. But this was a different sort of kiss than the one at the ball—warm, tender, persuasive.

He turned his lips to her cheek and kissed his way down her jaw, to her neck. She gasped at the pleasure he gave her. A honeymoon in Provence with Simon...

But a *marriage* to Simon? A *lifetime* with him?

But oh... his lips on her neck made her shiver.

He couldn't possibly love her, at least not the way she'd adored him for so long. This was too great a transformation from how callously he'd treated her at Lady Chilcombe's.

"I suppose," she said, "four weeks of you teaching me how to make love will be useful. If I decide not to marry you, if I can go on the stage—goodness, even if I did marry you. Well, I read the scandal sheets behind Mama's back. Even as a duchess, there would be men trying it on with me."

He pulled away from her, his brows furrowed in a puzzled frown.

She was hard pressed to fight the glee rising in her. "Thank you, Simon. It is better to know, to have a taste of what a man—"

"You minx." A grin split his face. "I'll give you a taste, but it will take a lifetime to feast at the whole banquet."

The kiss that followed was long and thorough and had her melting inside before he returned his attentions to her neck.

This was a sample of heaven and she wished it could go on forever, but...

"Why, Simon?" She had to know. "Why me? Why now? I thought you and Miss Hazelton—"

"No." He pulled back and looked at her. "Miss Hazelton? Never. But you... I've known you forever. Won't you please say you'll be my duchess?"

His duchess. The words sent a frisson of foolish longing through her.

"Before you answer, you must stop distracting me and let me finish my story about the Swilling Duke." He cast a lascivious gaze over her, and she felt her cheeks heating. "And perhaps..." he touched a finger to her nose, "you ought to tell me all about my friend's sweet little sister, the one who followed me around, who grew up to be a beautiful, spirited woman."

"The one who was a complete pea goose?"

"Your brother says you fancied yourself in love with me. Can you not fall in love with me again? Or... is there someone else?"

She dropped her gaze.

"I had other tendres—I did."

Tendres. Not love, nothing like what she'd felt for Simon. What she still felt for him, if she was being honest. It had only, always and forever, been Simon.

"I could never have married them. I didn't love them."

Even though she'd come to accept that Simon had no interest in her, she still wouldn't marry without true love.

"I'd met Sally at school, and wondered if I could act, on the stage, at least for a while. Before I could get up the courage to raise the subject with my parents, Papa died, Mama was grieving, and Fitz fell apart for a while. Fitz and George married, Cass met Saulsfield, and, well, I had to face the Season all alone except for Mama's company. When I ran into you in the passageway at the ball, I thought, 'thank heavens, here is Simon.'"

He shook his head and dropped a brief kiss on her lips. "Here is Simon, the jug-bitten, bacon-brained, Swilling Duke."

Despite her determination to be stern, she smiled. "As you proved to be."

"Do you know what I saw in that passageway at Lady Chilcombe's?"

Go back and tell Percy we've had our tumble if you will, and demand payment from him. "Yes of course; you told me. You saw a prostitute who'd wandered in through the servants' entrance."

One strong arm slid under her knees and the other around her shoulder, making her gasp.

"You may box my ears," he said, "but let me explain first."

He carried her to a wingchair near the hearth and sat down, cradling her head on his wide shoulder. His chest hair tickled her nose. She held back a sneeze and set her hand tentatively on his bare shoulder.

His hand came down over hers before she could explore the alien surface.

"I'll start at the beginning. I was an only child," he said, and he told her about losing his parents, about his love for Loughton Manor and the Lovelace family.

"I remember. You would arrive looking sad, and by the end of the visit, you were as big a nincompoop as any Lovelace boy."

With a laugh, he kissed her nose and went on. Though he touched on his military career, he glossed over his time on campaign in the Peninsula, later at Waterloo, and later still in India and the Americas.

"You're well-traveled," she said, "I envy you."

"One day, I'll tell you more about Spain and the other places, and you won't."

When it came to the news of the dukedom, he spoke of his wild swings of emotion and his reluctant decision to seek a girl with a rich dowry, and then he paused.

"My behavior the night of the ball was not my finest hour, I'm afraid."

Then he told her about encountering two well-dressed women on the street in front of a house across the square from Lady Chilcombe's. The resident there, a friend of Simon's companion that night, was holding a party for his bachelor friends.

She remembered that party. "I saw gentlemen and a group of ladies from the carriage window as they were gathering and wondered."

"Yes, well, I stayed for a drink only. Or perhaps more than one. I did not, er—forgive the boldness, my dear, but when confessing one's sins, one should be honest. I did not partake of the company. My friend, however, stayed longer and came along to the ball a bit later."

"Sir Percy. I suppose he participated in the orgy."

He froze. "I did not say a name. And how on earth would you know of such—"

"Girls whisper too. And you told me to 'go back and tell Percy', remember?"

With a sigh, he went on. "When I saw you..." Fingers swept through her soggy hair. "It was the golden hair and the blue eyes, and the... the..."

"Bold manner?"

"No. Well, I was told the young virgins would never put themselves forward, lest some dragon of a chaperone breathe fire at them."

Nancy stared into the hearth flames, remembering that night. No one had seen them in the passageway, but later, yes, people had seen her try to confront him. Mother had quietly dressed her down after.

What he'd said to her later had been reprehensible. What he'd done... casting up his accounts had embarrassed her, but it must have thoroughly shamed him. That was the part the scandal sheets focused on.

The passionate kiss in the passageway had been like nothing she'd ever experienced before.

"I'm peckish." He tucked a lock of her hair behind her ear. "Are you? Shall we return to the table?"

His hand paused and then his fingers began to knead her scalp in a mesmerizing rhythm.

"I am probably hungry. Probably starving in fact. But... would you kiss me again? Another real kiss, Simon. Like the one you gave me when you thought I was a soiled d—"

His lips came down on her open mouth. She giggled, allowing him entrance, and then pulling his head closer.

While he nipped and their lips moved together, she explored. She'd lived all her life with brothers, yet a man's body was foreign territory, a revelation that had ripples of heat running through her, making her yearn for something more, something as yet unknown, whatever it was that made women throw all good sense aside.

She smoothed a hand up to his neck and his ardor increased. His hair, thick and soft, was already almost dry. Scruff covered his cheeks and his jaw, but the strong cords of his neck were firm skin over muscle. Her fingers traveled over powerful shoulders and raked though the scant hair covering his taut chest.

He drew away from her, so close she could see each whisker of his beard, his eyes glowing darkly, a wicked smile forming.

"What else would you like me to do?"

"Oh." Her heart swelled and pressed against her

lungs as she gulped for breath. *Everything*, she thought, but the word wouldn't come.

He was fumbling with her neckcloth, one-handed then. The poorly tied knot dissolved. He tossed the bit of linen away, then kissed her again while he helped her wriggle out of her coats.

Cool air touched her back as warm fingers swirled up her spine and around and... Ah. He was cupping her breast, stroking the nipple. Ribbons of pleasure unfurled in her, coursed through her middle, echoed in the place between her legs.

"All right?" he murmured.

She felt herself nod.

He went back to kissing her, easing the shirt up, up, up. Breaking the kiss, he tore the shirt over her head, tossed it, and then paused.

She was as half-naked as he was. She looked down at her bare breasts and a wave of sheer wantonness came over her. When she raised her gaze, she found him focused upon her face, a grim set to his mouth. Not anger; he looked like he was holding the reins of a breakaway horse.

"Yes?" he asked.

What was he asking? She wasn't sure, she only knew she didn't want him to stop.

You'll go to the altar an innocent virgin, he'd said, *but not an ignorant one.*

She wanted to know, but one way or another, she'd be sealing her fate, wouldn't she?

A night with Simon. If he truly would marry her, a lifetime of nights with him…

"Yes."

"And you'll give me four weeks?" His long fingers swirled around each breast, addling her brain.

Four weeks. That meant she couldn't leave tonight.

"You'll take me to Birmingham?"

"I promise. Word of honor. We'll leave tomorrow after breakfast."

His hand was doing magical things.

"Stay with me tonight," she said.

"I wouldn't dream of leaving."

* * *

"I HOPE YOU ARE RIGHT." THOUGH LADY NEDA Loughton was a full head shorter than her eldest, Fitz hurried to keep up with her furious pace.

Dawn lit the sky in the east and the grass, wet from a night of rain, squished underfoot.

Mother had been up the whole night fretting and wondering when Simon would escort Nancy home, long after George had shepherded the little ones to the nursery, long after Mel and the rest of the family and guests had retired. Long after Sir Percy and Miss Hazelton had ceased casting up their accounts, and Fitz had turned the key on his brother, James, locking him in his room.

Fitz had sat up with Mother, insisting she wait until dawn for her invasion.

He suppressed a chuckle. He hoped it didn't turn into a siege.

"Who knew Nancy could be so defiant and stubborn?" he said.

If Mother hadn't dug in her heels over Sally Simpkins, there might have been no rebellion at all. He ought to have intervened.

He held his tongue though and said, "Simon likely needed the whole night to woo her."

"Yes. And I can imagine how he went about it. I was young once, you know."

"He'll marry her, Mother. And trust me, he won't take her maidenhead."

Or if he did, it wouldn't matter if they married soon. They could send for a special license, if need be.

"Just wait, Mama. She'll be in the bed, and he'll be on the sofa in the parlor."

She tossed a harumph and a dismissive look over her shoulder.

As far as Fitz was concerned, a betrothal was a license to make love. Simon, given the devilish temptation, might have done just what Fitz did in a moment of madness with his Mel. But Simon would have had a great deal more opposition from Nancy than Mel had offered Fitz.

Perhaps. Anything was possible.

"I'll get out the dueling pistols if needed," Fitz teased.

"You'll do no such thing."

"No. I suppose not." He trusted Simon to do the right thing, but if honor required it, he'd thrash him.

They made their way over the bridge and around the other side of the lake until they reached the garden surrounding the folly. In the damp dawn, the scent of roses filled the air.

He took out his key while his mother took in a long breath.

As it happened, the door was unlocked.

"I'll go first," he said.

"No." She pushed him aside. "You ought not to see your sister this way."

Fitz fought a smile, watching her indignant back as she entered. Nancy, the youngest and most congenial of the girls, would always be first in Mother's heart. Once one knew that, everything was easy to understand.

Inside, it took a moment for his vision to adjust. The candles had burned down. A fire had been lit but that had burned down as well.

And there—he'd been wrong on both counts. Wrapped in a blanket on the carpet in front of the hearth, Simon lay fast asleep, his arms around a sleeping Nancy.

Simon's arm was bare, but Nancy was dressed. Somewhat dressed. Her arm bore a white sleeve that looked more like part of a boy's shirt than the sleeve of a lady's chemise.

Her skirts and his shirt from the night before hung over chairs, drying.

Both looked peaceful.

Mother turned a troubled gaze up at him. "They shall marry immediately."

A TENDER CARESS OF HER BREAST STIRRED DELICIOUS sensations, rousing Nancy from sleep. Dim light filtered around the closed curtains, signaling daybreak. She turned her head, and her lips were captured in a kiss so intense it sent heat pouring through her and brought her fully awake. Her thoughts raced back over the scant hours before and Simon's lessons in lovemaking, and she rolled on her side facing him. Her fingers retraced the planes of his back and stroked down over the firm muscles of his bottom and thighs still encased in the trousers he'd refused to remove. Daringly, she slipped her hand between them and gasped at the hard length of him.

He clapped a hand over hers. "No," he said, his voice gravelly and tight. "At least not until we're wed."

A fuzzy part of her brain considered and rejected the delay. "Must we wait?"

In the long pause ensued, she saw desire warring with his determination to wait.

Impatience, annoyance flared in her. Before exhaustion had claimed her, he'd brought her to eye-opening ecstasy more than once. Yet he'd abstained from that pleasure himself. She knew enough to know there was more.

She freed her hand and raked a nail through his bristly jaw. "Marriage is the price you'll exact for all the pleasures of the flesh? For you as well?" she prodded.

"It's not a price. It won't be a price. It won't be forced. I want you to know me first, I want you to choose."

"And if I choose now?"

"I want you to choose more than one night of making love. I want a lifetime with you. A family. Happiness."

Her hand stilled. *A lifetime.* The full gravity of what he was asking hit her. He was asking—and offering—much more than girlish fantasies of romance and the sensual pleasures he'd introduced her to. He wanted a marriage like that of her parents before Papa died, like George's marriage to Sophie, and Fitz's marriage to Mel. He wanted happiness.

Could it be true? Could she trust him?

"I love you, Nancy."

Hope soared in her, but before she could speak, they heard noises outside.

"I'll go first," a muffled man's voice said.

Alarm coursed through her. That, she was sure, was Fitz.

"No. You mustn't see your sister this way."

Mother was here too. She ought to have expected it.

Nancy rolled onto her back and closed her eyes.

The doorknob rattled and a gust of moist air kissed her cheek.

Mother's indrawn breath shattered the silence. 'They shall marry immediately," she said, her voice tight.

"Yes. Or I shall shoot him."

The amusement in Fitz's voice told Nancy he'd do no such thing.

Simon squeezed her side and stirred. The blanket shifted as he sat up and wished Mother and Fitz a sleepy good morning.

"Think of it, Mother," Fitz said. "Our Nancy, a duchess."

Simon shuffled around, getting to his feet. "My shirt's finally dry," he said blandly.

Nancy barely swallowed a giggle. Mother must be getting a shocked eyeful of Simon's bare chest and tight trousers.

"Beg pardon," Simon said. "Yes. I will marry Nancy, if she'll have me."

"She'll have you," Fitz said.

A grumble rose in Nancy's throat at Fitz's high-handedness. Simon said she'd have a choice.

She decided to feign sleep and hear what her erstwhile intended had to say.

"I believe I sent over some tea," Fitz said. "If we can heat some water."

"I fetched some from the cistern last night." Simon shuffled around, and opening her eyes a slit, she saw him stirring the fire and hanging a pot.

"Waited on by a duke," Fitz murmured.

Long moments passed in silence as chairs shifted and dishes clinked. Mother's skirts swished as she bustled around; chairs creaked, silverware tinkled, and Simon murmured "only sugar."

"A common license, I think," Mother said. "You may ride to the bishop today."

Desire warred with worry. A common license meant that, in a mere seven days, she'd be married.

"With my utmost respect, my lady," Simon said, "no. Nancy and I have talked. I will court her. We will call the banns. Meanwhile, I will escort her to Birmingham to see my property near there and to visit her friend. We will need a chaperone, and I would like that person to be you, Lady Loughton."

Heart soaring, Nancy held her breath through the silence that followed.

"If," Simon continued, "after our courtship, Nancy is *willing* to marry, we'll have the wedding here, and then travel on to the south of France for our honeymoon. I have a villa there."

"And if she isn't willing?" Mother's voice trembled with indignation.

"She may cry off." Simon said. "It will give her time to know that... to know that I truly do care for her. She may give me my congé, but I feel hopeful she won't."

"Well-played, Swillingstone," Fitz said.

"I'm not playing, Loughton. I love Nancy." A loud thud followed, like a fist hitting the table.

"Simon." Nancy emerged from the twisted blankets. No matter how jumbled her emotions, she'd best intervene before fists flew in earnest.

She clutched the front of her shirt closed and brushed a hand over her tangled hair. It must be writhing about like Medusa's mane, but there was nought she could about it now. At least the shirt she'd borrowed from James covered her almost to her knees and her trousers still covered the rest.

While Mother's frown deepened, and Fitz pressed his lips on what she could see would be a grin, Simon escorted her to the table and made her a cup of tea. When she pushed a lock of hair back, the shirt flapped open. Mother's eyes narrowed on a spot on her neck that Simon had given particular attention last night, and this time Fitz did chuckle. She hurriedly pulled the shirt flaps together over what must be a spot chafed by Simon's beard.

"I was just asking your mother if she'd chaperone us when we visit Marston Green," Simon said oblivious to the reactions of her family.

Nancy nodded. She wasn't oblivious—couldn't afford to be, if she was truly to have a choice as Simon promised.

"Good morning, Mama. Fitz. Now you are here, I suppose we must talk. Firstly, you must know that Simon has been a perfect gentleman. I am still a virgin."

Mother gasped and color rose in her cheeks. No doubt she had a different idea of what constituted gentlemanly behavior.

"And secondly, I am going to Birmingham with Simon. He has promised I'll be chaperoned, but if you don't wish to come, Mama, perhaps Mr. Smith can hire a genteel lady to accompany us."

"Of course," Fitz said. "The plan is eminently sensible. You'll both go to Birmingham and Mother will go with you, won't you, Mother?"

She felt the squeeze of Simon's hand, realizing she'd reached for him. He beamed a smile at her, and she couldn't help but smile back.

"We can travel there today and arrive before nightfall," Simon said. "What say you, Nancy?"

He was asking her. Giving her a choice.

It was the journey she'd planned for this day anyway, though what she'd contemplated would have been far less comfortable. Not to mention, she'd have been missing the company of a handsome duke.

"*Nancy*," her mother prodded.

Her mother would be there as well, keeping her from falling head over ears into the soup with Simon. So once the last banns had been read, she'd have a choice.

She knew what her choice would be but she'd take him up on his offer of time to know him better.

Fitz stood. "Now, I understood you packed a bag and carried it over here yesterday. Have you a proper gown here?"

"I do."

"Then off you go and find it. Get dressed, and Mother will walk you home while Simon and I follow behind and speak about arrangements. If you're to leave this morning, we'll have to hurry."

When she stood, Simon jumped up and pressed a kiss to her cheek. "Until later," he said, a smile lighting his face.

Warmth bloomed, kindling memories of his touch and his tenderness the night before, of his kindness years earlier. She went up on her toes and pressed her lips to his ear. "I love you too, Simon."

"Nancy," mother chided.

Simon's arms engulfed her in a hug that was all too brief.

"Go and dress," he said.

"Is that an order, your grace?"

Simon blinked.

"Shall you spin me around and send me off with a slap on my bottom?" she whispered. "And say, 'get you gone'?"

His eyes flared and then he laughed, draping an arm over her shoulder and escorting her to the bedchamber door where he took both of her hands and raised them to his lips. "Minx," he whispered. "If it's a spanking you want, my love, I'll certainly oblige. But not in front of your mother and brother."

Mama stood frowning while Fitz's hand covered what she knew to be a smile. With a parting kiss, she slipped through the door to dress for the first day of her new role as Simon's beloved.

EPILOGUE

*T*he pews of the village church were all but bursting with people of all ages and classes, each in his or her finest attire, including a few old friends in their regimentals. Sir Percy's head poked above the others, bleary-eyed, seated next to his new lady, the former Miss Hazelton. Mrs. Simpkins and Sally were here as well, crowded in with Lovelaces in one of the family pews.

"She'll be here," George murmured.

Simon stamped down on his anxiety and stood at parade rest.

There'd been no sign of bridal nerves from Nancy; he was the jumpy one. Not reluctant, no, not that. After four weeks of curbing his desires, he was chomping at the bit for the wedding night. Or the wedding afternoon.

Lady Loughton had proved to be a formidable chaperone. They'd had no further opportunities for anything more than a few chaste kisses. He'd stayed the last few nights at the Swan, riding out to Loughton Manor daily through the sweet smell of hay being scythed in the fields.

Rain—a sign of good luck, George had assured him—had freed the locals from haying this day so they could attend the wedding and fêting of one of their favorites, the Honorable Nancy Lovelace.

She was his favorite as well.

The organist began a march, the congregation stirred, and Rupert Lovelace entered, escorting his mother to a front pew, where she joined George's wife, Sophie, and the boys of Nancy's Midsummer Night's caper brigade. The second and third pews overflowed with other Lovelace siblings and their spouses and children.

Then Mary came down the aisle, carrying a basket of rose petals. He chuckled remembering the basket of rose hips Nancy had gathered to prepare the itching powder.

Fitz's wife, Mel, the bride's only other attendant, entered. And then everyone stood.

His bride advanced on Fitz's arm, her eyes

luminous against the pale pink of her bonnet and frock, her cheeks rosy, her smile shy.

Heart bursting, speechless, Simon accepted her hand, and the ceremony proceeded in a blur of high emotion that carried them all the way through the wedding breakfast for the locals at the village assembly rooms, and the family event that followed at Loughton Manor.

Then they were seated on the lowly cushioned bed of a freshly painted narrow cart, with streamers and rattling tins flowing behind. The family's coachman took the reins and drove them, bouncing and laughing, over the hurriedly completed bridge, dropping them in the sea of red and pink roses surrounding the folly.

They would spend their wedding night here and depart for the ducal yacht and France the next day.

Simon lifted her and carried her over the threshold.

"Where it all began," she whispered.

"No." He settled her to her feet and pulled her close. "It began long before that, my girl. It began in the music room with you playing a song about sheep." He smiled. "I had to wait for you to grow up."

"And I have." She pulled his head down. "Now, teach me the rest. Make love to me."

And he did.

The End

If you're so inclined, please consider leaving a review at Goodreads, Bookbub, or the bookseller of your choice, and thank you!

A NOTE FROM THE AUTHOR

I hope you've enjoyed Nancy's and Simon's story, which is part of a multi-author collection of stand-alone romances called Revenge of the Wallflowers.

If you've read any of my other books, you may recognize the two Loughton brothers, Fitz and George, as the heroes of *The Impetuous Heiress* and *Convincing the Countess*, two books in my Upstart Christmas Brides series.

At present, I'm in the early stages of a story due out in November 2025 involving the dowager Lady Neda Loughton's widowed friend, Lady Chilcombe. I'm also mulling a future project involving Neda herself. We'll see how that goes!

Many thanks go to my author friends at the Bluestocking Belles. Their encouragement, support, and expertise in the craft of writing as well as all things Regency are invaluable. Thanks also go to editor Tessa Shapcott, who provided insightful guidance on the story and spotted all my pesky Americanisms.

And thank you to you, Dear Reader, for your support of my books. I hope I've given you a few hours of enjoyable escape from our 21st century.

Alina K. Field

BOOKS BY ALINA K. FIELD

SONS OF THE SPY LORD SERIES

MARRYING MR. GIBSON

Previously titled *The Bastard's Iberian Bride*

Paulette Heardwyn rushes to visit her dying guardian, set
on learning the truth about her father. But the only man
with answers takes his secrets to the grave, leaving her
penniless—unless she marries his illegitimate son.

https://alinakfield.com/book/marrying-mr-gibson/

THE VISCOUNT'S SEDUCTION

Lady Sirena Hollister has lost everything, even her fey
abilities. But when the fairies hand her a chance at a
London Season, her schemes for revenge stir up an
unknown enemy, and spark danger of a different sort, in
the person of a handsome Viscount.

https://alinakfield.com/book/the-viscounts-seduction/

THE ROGUE'S LAST SCANDAL

Falling—literally—into the arms of the *ton*'s most
outrageous rogue seems a risky path of escape, but Maria
Graciela Kingsley y Romero has no other choice. Only
England's greatest spy lord can help her, and he is not to
be found—so his son will have to do!

https://alinakfield.com/book/rogues-last-scandal/

THE COUNTERFEIT LADY

Vowing she'll never submit to an arranged marriage, an earl's daughter bolts for the seaside cottage that will someday be hers. But she finds her quiet refuge occupied by the last man she ever wants to see—an American artist, who's also a thief. And quite possibly one of her father's spies.

https://alinakfield.com/book/the-counterfeit-lady/

AVENGING THE EARL'S LADY

The long war is over, but honor requires vanquishing one last enemy, and the Earl of Shaldon has no time for romance. But when the lady he longs for interferes in his plot, and his enemy strikes at her, nothing else matters but avenging his lady.

https://alinakfield.com/book/avenging-the-earls-lady/

NOVELLAS AND HOLIDAY STORIES: THE MARQUESS AND THE MIDWIFE

Finalist, 2016 National Reader's Choice Award

Uncovering a lie drives a new marquess back from a self-imposed exile at Christmas to find the only woman he's ever loved. Finding her turns out to be easy, uncovering her stunning secrets, a bit harder. But winning her back will be the greatest challenge of all.

https://alinakfield.com/book/the-marquess-and-the-midwife/

A LEAP INTO LOVE

Can a gentleman be too charming?

The ladies of Upper Upton think so.

When the single ladies of the village conspire to teach their charmer a lesson that might bankrupt him, the town's loveliest young widow—who's sworn off marriage forever—steps up to warn him.

https://alinakfield.com/book/a-leap-into-love/

LILIANA'S LETTER: FINALIST, 2015 NATIONAL READER'S CHOICE AWARD

The Matchmaker Meets the Matchbreaker

Liliana Ashford's future as a professional chaperone depends on her wealthy charge's successful marriage, but her own close encounter with a scoundrel years ago makes her determined to save the girl from the same kind of rogue.

https://alinakfield.com/book/lilianas-letter/

THE GHOST OF DEPFORD HALL

A sweet Halloween short story

It's her mother's last All Hallows' Eve.

When family, friends, and tenants gather, goblins, ghouls, and ghosts are banned from this All Hallows' Eve party.

Only, no one told the Ghost of Depford Hall!

https://alinakfield.com/book/ghost-depford-hall/

COURTED BY THE EARL: PREVIOUSLY TITLED BELLA'S BAND

A 2015 RONE Award Finalist

Saddled with his brother's title and debts, nothing about this new life makes the Earl of Hackwell want to stay—until he meets a lady with a secret that can change everything.

https://alinakfield.com/book/courted-by-the-earl/

ROSALYN'S RING: 2014 BOOK BUYER'S BEST WINNER, NOVELLA CATEGORY

Done with grieving her losses, a late nobleman's daughter has fallen into a tidy spinster's life in London. But when one snowy Christmas Eve, a young woman needs rescue, she seizes the chance to do good—and to recover a family heirloom that ought to be hers.

https://alinakfield.com/book/rosalyns-ring/

HAUNTING MISS FENWICK

Thrilled to finally have a permanent home, a Squire's daughter won't let a supernatural creature scare her away. While hunting the ghost she doesn't believe in, she stumbles upon a mysterious flesh and blood man who might be the key to all of her problems.

https://alinakfield.com/book/haunting-miss-fenwick/

LADY TWISDEN'S PICTURE PERFECT MATCH

Promised York's marriage mart and the hospitality of his cousin's doddering stepmother, Major August Kellborn is shocked to find that his fetching hostess is the one woman who stirs his heart.

https://alinakfield.com/book/lady-twisdens-picture-perfect-match/

FLOWERS FOR HIS LADY

Eleanor Gurnwood has only one goal in sight: to make this year's Christmas service beautiful for the parishioners of St. Tancred's—until the Christmas eve when a man from her past rides in on a white horse.

https://alinakfield.com/book/flowers-for-his-lady/

UNDER THE CHAMPAGNE MOON

Homeless and living on the charity of her former guardian, Fleur Hardouin's heart longs for Captain Gareth Ardleigh, whose kindness to her as a child she's never forgotten, but she needs an advantageous marriage.

Gareth has promised to find Fleur—on behalf of another man. Now he must choose between honoring a promise and trying to win the hand of the woman he loves.

https://alinakfield.com/book/under-the-champagne-moon/

The Upstart Christmas Brides Series

THE DUKE SHE DESPISED

Hiding her true identity, a young vicar's widow takes a position as housekeeper in a remote Scottish castle at Christmas for a new duke who years ago sabotaged her chance for happiness. She quickly falls for the duke's charming but not very competent factor, not knowing that he's hiding something also—he's the duke she despised!

https://alinakfield.com/book/the-duke-she-despised/

CONVINCING THE COUNTESS

A penniless widowed countess with trade in her blood

descends upon the country manor of her sons' negligent guardian, intent on confronting him about her boys' futures. Instead, she finds his younger brother, a business-minded aristocrat with a penchant for widows and a distaste for emotional entanglements. A man who once witnessed her greatest humiliation. A man offering enticing distractions that threaten to derail all her plans.

https://alinakfield.com/book/convincing-the-countess/

THE IMPETUOUS HEIRESS

Before dashing Lord Loughton can make amends with his neglected fiancée, the lady's meddling cousin delivers her to his doorstep. He soon realizes more is amiss than his carelessness. Can he uncover her secrets and win her back before he loses her altogether?

https://alinakfield.com/book/the-impetuous-heiress/

THE NABOB'S DESIGNING DAUGHTER

Ripped from his prestigious London practice to deliver a Highland duke's heir, a young doctor finds there are more snares awaiting than a risky birth, including a surprise—and worthless—bequest. There's also his best friend's cousin, who's blossomed from mousey to heart-stirringly beautiful, with enough wiles to convince an ambitious man that his heart belongs in the Highlands.

https://alinakfield.com/book/the-nabobs-designing-daughter/

THE EARL'S SCOTTISH HOYDEN

Coerced by her brother to spend an English Christmas at the country estate of the handsome but cold earl who all but jilted her a year earlier, Edme Beecham is determined to do no more than assist her brother in his business negotiations with the earl, and by all means, to protect her heart.

https://alinakfield.com/book/the-earls-scottish-hoyden/

THE MACBETH SERIES: FATED HEARTS

A Love After All Retelling of the Scottish Play

A Scottish Baron returning from two decades at war meets the wife he divorced and the daughter he disavowed before she was born, only to learn that everything he'd believed was a lie. Determined to win back the only woman he's ever loved he must first face the viper who drove them apart.

https://alinakfield.com/book/fated-hearts/

THE COMTESSE OF MIDNIGHT

A Scottish Earl on a quest for the elusive Comtesse de Fontenay, rescues a French lady smuggler during a devastating storm, taking shelter with her. As the stormy night drags on, he suspects she knows the lady he's seeking, the lady who holds the secret to his identity.

https://alinakfield.com/book/the-comtesse-of-midnight/

CLAIMS OF THE HEART

Since a perilous fall, Lucie Macbeth has been seeing more than a settled future as the heiress to a Scottish barony. The visions plaguing her include a man—one far above her class and breeding, and English to boot. He's engaged to a duke's granddaughter as well, and thus wholly inappropriate. Though she can't marry him, and she won't become any man's leman, when the Sight warns her of danger to him, her conscience, and her heart tell her she can't walk away.

https://alinakfield.com/book/claims-of-the-heart/

www.ingramcontent.com/pod-product-compliance
Lightning Source LLC
Chambersburg PA
CBHW061200170626
46809CB00003B/1190

* 9 7 8 1 9 4 4 0 6 3 4 5 0 *